Wilfred Whitten, John Greenleaf Whittier

John G. Whittier

A biographical sketch

Wilfred Whitten, John Greenleaf Whittier

John G. Whittier
A biographical sketch

ISBN/EAN: 9783337388546

Printed in Europe, USA, Canada, Australia, Japan

Cover: Foto ©Raphael Reischuk / pixelio.de

More available books at **www.hansebooks.com**

JOHN G. WHITTIER

A BIOGRAPHICAL SKETCH.

BY

WILFRED WHITTEN.

LONDON :

EDWARD HICKS, Jr.,

14, BISHOPSGATE WITHOUT, AND 2, AMEN CORNER.

1892.

HEADLEY BROS
INVICTA PRINTING WORKS
INVICTA
ASHFORD·KENT

CONTENTS.

JOHN G.WHITTIER

CHAPTER I.

NEW ENGLAND ANCESTRY.

"And let us hope, as well we can,
That the silent angel who garners man
May find some grain as of old he found
In the human cornfield ripe and sound,
And the Lord of the Harvest deign to own
The precious seed by the fathers sown!"

"The Prophecy of Samuel Sewall."

"The firm endurance of suffering by the martyrs of conscience, if it be rightly contemplated, is the most consolatory spectacle in the crowded life of man . . . . of all destinies it is that which most exalts the sect or party whom it visits, and bestows on their story an undying command over the hearts of their fellow men."

Sir James Mackintosh.

THE story of John Greenleaf Whittier falls into a simple but glowing narrative, and the chief concern of the writer is that he may not fail in that reverent handling due to the

finished labour and sorrows of a good man. Our
poet's entreaty for the balm of men's forget-
fulness cannot be set aside without hesitation,
although gently set aside it must be for the
sake of the human family from which he has
been withdrawn—

> O living friends who love me,
> O dear ones gone above me,
> Careless of other fame
> I leave to you my name,
> Hide it from idle praises,
> Save it from evil phrases ;
> Why, when dear lips that spake it
> Are dumb, should strangers wake it ?

The ancestry of Whittier is interesting. The
first member of his family who sought a home in
America was Thomas Whittier, who, in 1638, took
his passage to Boston, Mass., in the "Confidence,"
the vessel sailing from Southampton under one
John Jobson. Thomas Whittier was but a youth
of eighteen when he adventurously left the
old country, but he fortunately had companion-
ship in a family of the name of Rolfe, with which
he subsequently became connected by marriage.

In 1645 we find him settled with his bride at Salisbury, a small place near the mouth of the Merrimac River. He also lived at Newbury, and then, in 1648, came to live at Haverhill, eleven miles south-west of Salisbury. The local records reveal the curious fact that Thomas Whittier brought with his other goods and chattels the first hive of bees known to the settlement, and a clever writer has seen in the circumstance a fancied kinship with the story of the bees swarming about the baby lips of Pindar, sweetest of Greek, as Whittier was of American poets. Thomas Whittier lived long and in good report ; he died in 1696, and his wife in 1710. Ten out of eleven children survived their parents, and it was from the youngest, Joseph, the poet had his descent. Joseph Whittier first established the family connection with Quakerism by marrying, in 1694, the year in which George Fox's Journal was printed in London, Mary, daughter of Joseph Peasley. His death took place in 1739, and of his nine children it was again the youngest who became the ancestor of

the poet. Joseph Whittier, the younger, married
Sarah Greenleaf, of Newbury. Their tenth child,
John, married in 1804, Abigail Hussey, of
Somersworth, and the children of this union
were Mary; *John Greenleaf* (born Dec. 17, 1807);
Matthew Franklin ; and Elizabeth Hussey.

Such being the poet's ancestry, some
slight account of the conditions under which
these worthies lived will leave us free to
enter on the story of the man whose inborn
poetic fire we shall perhaps find to have been
kindled well nigh at the stake itself. Scarcely
in history is there a blacker story of persecu-
tion than that which marks the annals of New
England under the Puritan Fathers and their
descendants. Its incidents, says one of Whittier's
editors, " grate on the poet's memory, and fire
his indignation, and he refuses to be cajoled into
regarding as saintly religionists the rigid op-
pressors who wielded the scourge and the brand-
ing iron for Quakers, and at whose bidding
Friends male and female, dangled from gibbets."

In Whittier's verse the hatchet is never

quite buried. In the "King's Missive" the poet calls up the historic scene in which "the worshipful Governor Endicott, a grave, strong man, who knew no peer," was suddenly stayed in his cruel courses by the return from England of an exiled Friend, bearing the imperative order of Charles II. to stop "this vein of innocent blood." Little suspecting the man came thus weaponed, Endicott cried in his anger—

> "At every turn
> The pestilent Quakers are in my path !
> Some we have scourged, and banished some,
> Some hanged, more doomed, and still they come,
> Fast as the tide of yon bay sets in,
> Sowing their heresy's seed of sin."

> o   o   o

> Twice and thrice on the chamber floor,
>   Striding fiercely from wall to wall,
> " The Lord do so to me and more,"
>   The governor cried, "if I hang not all
> Bring hither the Quaker." Calm, sedate,
> With the look of a man at ease with fate,
> Into that presence, grim and dread,
> Came Samuel Shattuck, with hat on head.

"Off with the knave's hat!"　An angry hand
　Smote down the offence ; but the wearer said,
With a quiet smile, " By the king's command
　I bear this message and stand in his stead."
In the Governor's hand a missive he laid
With the royal arms on its seal displayed,
And the proud man spake as he gazed thereat,
Uncovering, " Give Mr. Shattuck his hat."

He turned to the Quaker, bowing low,—
　" The king commandeth your friends' release,
Doubt not he shall be obeyed, although
　To his subjects' sorrow and sin's increase.
What he here enjoineth, John Endicott,
His loyal servant, questioneth not.
You are free ! God grant the spirit you own
May take you from us to parts unknown."

Although this stopped hangings on Boston
Common (already there had been three), it did not
abrogate the laws which wreaked themselves on
Friends in fines, whippings, banishment and
prison-bars.　Only a year after these events it
was enacted that any master of a vessel who "imported" a Quaker should be liable to a fine of 5,000
pounds of tobacco.　Whoever went to a Quaker's
meeting was to pay 10/-, and £5 if he preached.
Quakers not inhabitants were to be banished, and

flogged if they returned; and if they were inhabitants they must be banished or recant. Travelling Quakers were to be whipped through the towns. And when, at last, the penal statutes against heresy were allowed to rest, the old hatred smouldered on for generations; "time," says an American biographer of Whittier, "softened the hearts of bigots, and wore off the sharp edges of dogmas; but this was not until Church and State had been divorced, and not until the Quaker's memory of the days of bitterness had become as unchanging as his sad-coloured garments."

It imported nothing to Whittier that his immediate ancestors had perhaps escaped the lash and halter. Through them he had none the less touch with the Boston persecutions, and he inherited that in his blood which broke out again and again in fierce hatred of tyranny and intolerance, past and present. The children of Thomas Whittier, the immigrant, were probably Friends, and we have seen that the youngest, Joseph, married into the Peasley family. Joseph

Peasley was much associated with Thomas Macey (both being preaching Friends), and one of the family traditions tells how, in 1659, the latter sturdy Quaker fell under the law.

Four Friends from Salem were visiting the small towns along the shores of the Merrimac, and it is probable that Thomas Whittier and his family heard them gladly when in due course they came to Haverhill. Thence they travelled to Salisbury, where Thomas Macey entertained them at his cottage after the simple apostolic manner of Friends. He was at once prosecuted, and ordered to pay thirty shillings, but, acting no doubt with wisdom, he fled to Nantucket, where he established himself. The story in detail is the subject of Whittier's stirring ballad, "The Exiles," in which we learn how, when Macey's pious guests were scarce seated,

> A heavy tramp of horses' feet
> Came sounding up the lane,
> And half a score of horse, or more,
> Came plunging through the rain.

Now, Goodman Macey, ope thy door—
We would not be housebreakers ;
A rueful deed thou'st done this day
In harbouring banished Quakers.

The escape of the Maceys, man and wife, by
leaping into a moored boat, and the dialogue
between them and their angry pursuers left on
the bank, are told vigorously and with humour—

The priest came panting to the shore—
His grave cocked hat was gone ;
Behind him, like some owl's nest, hung
His wig upon a thorn.

"Come back—come back!" the parson cried
"The Church's curse beware."
"Curse, an' thou wilt," said Macey, "but
Thy blessing prithee spare."

"Vile scoffer!" cried the baffled priest,
"Thou'lt yet the gallows see."
"Who's born to be hanged will not be drowned,"
Quoth Macey, merrily.

After some verses descriptive of the voyage
we learn—

Far round the bleak and stormy Cape
The vent'rous Macey passed,
And on Nantucket's naked isle
Drew up his boat at last.

And how, in log-built cabin,
   They braved the rough sea-weather ;
And there, in peace and quietness,
   Went down life's vale together :

How others drew around them,
   And how their fishing sped,
Until to every wind of heaven
   Nantucket's sails were spread ;

How pale Want alternated
   With Plenty's golden smile ;
Behold, is it not written
   In the annals of the isle ?

Whittier's young mind was fed with such stories, and in the family circle, when the fire-glow shimmered on the faces he loved, the boy's thoughts were prophetic, though he knew it not, of strife, and songs of strife, to come. In "Snow-Bound" the poet tells us,

Our mother, while she turned her wheel,
   Or run the new knit stocking heel,
Told how the midnight hordes came down
   At midnight on Cocheco town.

      o   o   o

Then, haply, with a look more grave,
   And soberer tone, some tale she gave
From painful Sewel's ancient tome,
   Beloved in every Quaker home,
Of faith fire-winged with martyrdom.

Does not the last line seem born of the moment when the boy's eye, flashing in the innocence of indignation, was answered by his mother's smile as she thought of the years and what they might bring.

CHAPTER II.

THE OLD HOME.

"Dear heart !—the legend is not vain
Which lights that holy hearth again,
And calling back from care and pain,
    And death's funereal sadness,
Draws round its old familiar blaze
The clustering groups of happier days,
And lends to sober manhood's gaze
    A glimpse of childish gladness."

"To My Sister."

———

"It was the policy of the good old gentleman to make his children feel that home was the happiest place in the world ; and I value this delicious home feeling as one of the choicest gifts a parent can bestow."

WASHINGTON IRVING.

———

IT is the truism of truisms to say that the influence of the home is chief in the making of character. Within that sphere it is not word and deed only that, for good or evil, impress themselves on a child's waxen mind, but looks also, and veiled looks, habitual moods and assumed, silence and darkness as well as motherly talk and cheery lamps, books of course, and the meanest picture on the nursery wall, the morning and the evening hour, the family's unity or lack of it, and things impalpable and invisible, not of the wills, but flowing unawares from the settled dispositions of the parents. This is matter of knowledge, yet the *home making* of men is only beginning to be recognised as something more than a duty enjoined by Solomon, even an art to be reduced to its first principles like any other. Perhaps the time is near when a new scientific Biography will set itself to discover and illustrate those principles in a way that has not yet been attempted. Meanwhile they may be approached in the written lives of men whose days and years are visibly linked in one chain continuing back unbroken into the mysteries of their first years. This continuity is a marked characteristic of Whittier's life, and constitutes, perhaps, its peculiar charm for ourselves. In the man's tones there is ever the *timbre* of his boy-

hood's shouts; he harks back often to the
"green mirage of a simple life," now dwell-
ing fondly on—

> Old customs, habits, superstitions, fears,
> All that lies buried under fifty years.

now nursing a fond regret of vanished days—

> O for boyhood's time of June,
> Crowding years in one brief moon.

now drawing from the past inspiration instead
of sighs—

> The great eventful Present hides the Past; but through
>   the din
> Of its loud life hints and echoes from the life behind
>   steal in ;
> And the lore of home and fireside, and the legendary
>   rhyme,
> Make the task of duty lighter which the true man owes
>   his time.

or again solemnly weighing the treasures of
memory and hope against each other—

> Clasp, Angel of the backward look
>   And folded wings of ashen gray
>   And voice of echoes far away,
> The brazen covers of thy book ;
> The weird palimpsest old and vast

Wherein thou hid'st the spectral past ;
Where, closely mingling, pale and glow
The characters of joy and woe ;
The monographs of outlived years,
Or smile-illumed or dim with tears,
    Green hills of life that slope to death,
And haunts of home, whose vista'd trees
Shade off to mournful cypresses
    With the white amaranths underneath.
Even while I look, I can but heed
    The restless sands' incessant fall,
Importunate hours that hours succeed,
Each clamorous with its own sharp need,
    And duty keeping pace with all.
Shut down and clasp the heavy lids ;
I hear again the voice that bids
The dreamer leave his dream mid-way
For larger hopes and graver fears :
Life greatens in these later years,
The century's aloe flowers to-day !
Yet, haply, in some lull of life,
Some Truce of God which breaks its strife
The worldling's eyes shall gather dew,
    Dreaming in throngful city ways
Of winter joys his boyhood knew ;
And dear and early friends—the few
Who yet remain—shall pause to view
    These Flemish pictures of old days ;
Sit with me by the homestead hearth,
And stretch the hands of memory forth
    To warm them at the wood-fire's blaze !

And thanks untraced to lips unknown
Shall greet me like the odours blown
From unseen meadows newly mown,
Or lilies floating in some pond,
Wood-fringed, the wayside gaze beyond ;
The traveller owns the grateful sense
Of sweetness near, he knows not whence,
And, pausing, takes with forehead bare
The benediction of the air.

The man who could play Whittier's part,
in Whittier's times, and still turn naturally
to scenes and feelings like these to find himself must be pourtrayed mainly apart from
his public employments. A quarter of a century
ago, indeed, we should have discussed Whittier
as Patriot, Abolitionist, or Teacher, but now
we desire rather to realize the *Man*, in whom
these characters became conspicuous only as
passing events and temporary conditions drew
them into prominence. Now, we ask, not so
much for his newspaper record, as for his
history in the family, in friendship, in the
social circle, and, so far as we may rightly
ask for it, in the chamber of his own heart.

The Whittier home stood and still stands

in a peaceful valley of not unusual beauty.
F. H. Underwood, whose excellent biography
of Whittier had the poet's approval, has thus
written of it :—

"The Whittier house is more open to view
from the main road than it was sixty years
ago. The woods that hemmed it in have been
mostly cleared, enlarging greatly the fields of
pasture and meadow. The house faces southward, and in front is a grass plot, sloping to-
wards a small but faithful brook. Here on
this sunny slope it was that 'once a garden
smiled,' and at its western corner rose the tall
well-sweep, since displaced by the prosaic pump.
The little brook comes from a marshy tract on
a higher level, and gurgles pleasantly through
a narrow rock ravine in which are the rude
remains of a dam."

Of this brook, whose music seems to have
haunted him in after years as that of the
Bandusian fountain haunted the ear of Horace,
Whittier wrote in the "Barefoot Boy":—

Laughed the brook for my delight,
Through the day and through the night,
Whispering at the garden wall,
Talked with me from fall to fall.

And what the other stream has been to countless lovers of Horace—a place of refreshing pilgrimage—"Little Brook" has been to many a reader of the volume that contains "Maud Müller" and "The Countess." A magazine writer thus enthusiastically describes his visit,—"We lay on the grass and listened to its pleasant voice, and tried to imagine the poet, a rosy-cheeked, curly headed, "Barefoot Boy," dabbling in its clear waters. And we wished that the blessed gift of health might be granted him as in that happy time, "boyhood's time of June." The place was so lovely, the associations were so interesting, that we were loth to leave—the grass was so green, the brook so sweet-voiced. The air was full of warm delightful summer sounds;—the drowsy hum of bees, the shrill cry of the locust, the distant lowing of cows. We looked and listened, and dreamed dreams, and sang snatches of old song."

"The foliage," continues Mr. Underwood, "is rich and varied in the immediate vicinity, and the country is seen to consist of softly rounded elevations—broad and flattened domes —lovely in colour and relieved by charming groups of trees. Westward lies lake Kenoza, half obscured, half revealed, among clumps and thickets."

Kenoza! o'er no sweeter lake
   Shall morning break or noon-cloud sail,—
No fairer face than thine shall take
   The sunset's golden veil.

Long be it ere the tide of trade
   Shall break the harsh-resounding din
The quiet of thy banks of shade,
   And hills that fold thee in.

Still let thy woodlands hide the hare,
   The shy loon sound his trumpet-note,
Wing-weary from his fields of air,
   The wild-goose on thee float.

Thy peace rebuke our feverish stir,
   Thy beauty our deforming strife ;
Thy woods and waters minister
   The healing of their life.

And sinless Mirth, from care released,
   Behold, unawed, thy mirrored sky,
Smiling as smiled on Cana's feast
   The Master's loving eye.

And when the summer day grows dim,
   And light mists walk thy mimic sea,
Revive in us the thought of Him
   Who walked on Galilee !

Other features in the Haverhill landscape
are graphically depicted by Mr. Underwood—
the dimly seen pyramidal mass of Agamenticus,
the gorgeous tints of the foliage in autumn,
the tract of black bog south-east of the homestead ; but it is certain that, however skilful
a writer may be, he cannot hope by the most
exact description to impress different minds
with the same idea of a complex landscape.

We will turn therefore to more exact deline-
ations of the Whittier home itself. This is a low
brown wooden house standing close to the road.
It was built by Thomas Whittier some forty years
after he came to Haverhill, when he would seem
to have desired to replace the old log house
of his youth by a family roof tree that should

shelter his children's children. " Externally,"
says Mr. Underwood, " it has been somewhat
changed of late years, but within, it remains
substantially as it was in the period in which
" Snow Bound " was located. New clapboards
and window caps, as well as new outer doors
and sashes, all in fresh paint, have given the
old home a spruce modern look. But some of the
ancient carpentry remains, and there are still
in use quaint iron door handles, latches, and
hinges, which Puritan smiths hammered out
two centuries ago. Some of the original doors,
too dilapidated for service, are stored in an
outbuilding. The glass in the windows is
modern, except a few panes in the kitchen
and chambers. The sturdy chimney has been
newly topped, but its antiquity is evident
when its huge mass is seen in the open space
of the large back chamber. One sees that the
chimney was the central idea of a new settler's
home. The kitchen fire-place, once broad
enough to admit benches on either side, has
now been narrowed by rows of bricks, thereby

closing a curious cave of an oven buried in
the recess. The square front rooms are un-
changed. The marks of their century are on
every part of the work : strength and simplicity. The oaken beams, which a man of fair
height can touch with an upraised hand, are
fifteen inches square and as firm as when laid.
The wainscots and floors are well preserved.
At one end of the kitchen was a bedroom
known as the mother's room, but it was in
the west front room that our poet saw the
light. The small chamber overhead is the one
he occupied when a boy. A flight of well
worn steps leads up to it from the kitchen.
Above are the time-stained rafters and the
boards pierced with nail points which used to
glisten like powdered stars on frosty mornings.
Here it was, as the poet has told us, where,
on stormy nights,—

> We heard the loosened clapboards tost,
> The boards-nails snapping in the frost ;
> And on us through the unplastered wall,
> Felt the light-rifted snow-flakes fall.

"If our readers," continues Mr. Underwood, "can recall the parts of this description, and look upon this old farmhouse from a proper point without, it will be seen that if there were once more a garden in front, a tall well-sweep at the left, the barn and sheds in the rear, and if the oaks on every side were renewed—sturdier, thicker, nearer,—the place would be once more what it was when Whittier was a boy. . . No; the Whittier homestead is not beautiful as artists consider beauty; but sweet and tender memories render our eyes misty as we look upon it; and with such associations there comes a feeling which the artist of mere beauty can never create. The scene is quiet, unmodernized, near to aboriginal nature, and suggestive of a calm simplicity that asks for no admiration,—as if a segment of another century had survived the changes of time."

Such was the boy's home; let us try to people it with the old familiar faces. Whittier has already done this for us in his exquisite "Snow-

Bound " than which no more finished picture
of rural home life has enriched poetry since
Horace sang to Roman patricians of his
father's humble Venusian farm on the bright-
flowing Aufidus. Herrick truly has sung with
a more exquisite grace of country sights and
sounds — " hock-carts, wassails, wakes " — and
even of the social hour,

> When the hearth
> Smiles to itself and gilds the roof with mirth.

Burns, using a metre alien to his genius, has
charmed mankind with his " Cotter's Saturday
Night ; " yet " Snow-Bound " remains without
a rival in the language as a mirror of home-bred
delights. See the evening circle gather, heedless
of the " shrieking of the mindless wind,"—

> As night drew on, and, from the crest
> Of wooded knolls that ridged the west,
> The sun, a snow-blown traveller, sank
> From sight beneath the smothering bank,
> We piled, with care, our nightly stack
> Of wood against the chimney back—
> The oaken log, green, huge, and thick,
> And on its top the stout back-stick :
> The knotty forestick laid apart,

And filled between with curious art
The ragged brush ; then hovering near,
We watched the first red blaze appear,
Heard the sharp crackle, caught the gleam
On white-washed wall and sagging beam,
Until the old, rude-furnished room
Burst flower-like into rosy bloom ;
While radiant with a mimic flame
Outside the sparkling drift became,
And through the bare-boughed lilac tree
Our own warm hearth seemed blazing free.
The crane and pendent trammels showed,
The Turks' heads on the andiron glowed ;
While childish fancy prompt to tell
The meaning of the miracle,
Whispered the old rhyme : ' *Under the tree*,'
When fire outdoors burns merrily,
There the witches are making tea.'

Shut in from all the world without,
We sat the clean-winged hearth about,
Content to let the north-wind roar
In baffled rage at pane and door,
While the red logs before us beat
The frost-line back with tropic heat ;
And ever, when a louder blast
Shook beam and rafter as it passed,
The merrier up its roaring draught
The great throat of the chimney laughed,
The house-dog on his paws outspread
Laid to the fire his drowsy head,
The cat's dark silhouette on the wall

A couchant tiger's seemed to fall ;
And, for the winter fireside meet,
Between the andirons' straddling feet,
The mug of cider simmered slow,
The apples sputtered in a row,
And, close at hand, the basket stood
With nuts from brown October's wood.

Then began riddle-making and story telling. The father, " a prompt, decisive man,"
as the poet calls him, who had gone through
many adventures among Indians and trappers
in his youth, would drift into recollections of
these wilder days.—

Our father rode again his ride
On Memphremagog's wooded side ;
Sat down again to moose and samp
In trapper's hut and Indian camp ;
Lived o'er the old idyllic ease
Beneath St. François' hemlock trees ;
Again for him the moonlight shone
On Norman cap and bodiced zone ;
Again he heard the violin play
Which led the village dance away,
And mingled in its merry whirl
The grandam and the laughing girl.

The mother next told—

In her fitting phrase
So rich and picturesque and free

(The common unrhymed poetry
Of simple life and country ways)
The story of her early days,—
She made us welcome to her home ;
Old hearths grew wide to give us room ;
We stole with her a frightened look
At the grey wizard's conjuring book,
The fame whereof went far and wide
Through all the simple country-side ;
We heard the hawks at twilight play,
The boat-horn on Piscataqua,
The loon's weird laughter far away ;
We fished her little trout-brook, knew
What flowers in wood and meadow grew,
What sunny hillsides autumn-brown
She climbed to shake the ripe nuts down,
Saw where in sheltered cove and bay
The ducks' black squadron anchored lay,
And heard the wild-geese calling loud
Beneath the grey November cloud.
Then, haply, with a look more grave,
And soberer tone, some tale she gave
From painful Sewell's ancient tome,
Beloved in every Quaker home,
Of faith fire-winged by martyrdom,
Or Chalkley's Journal, old and quaint,—
Gentlest of skippers, rare sea-saint !—
Who, when the dreary calms prevailed,
And water-butt and bread-cask failed,
And cruel, hungry eyes pursued
His portly presence mad for food,

With dark hints muttered under breath
Of casting lots for life or death,
Offered, if Heaven withheld supplies,
To be himself the sacrifice.
Then suddenly, as if to save
The good man from his living grave,
A ripple on the water grew,
A school of porpoise flashed in view.
' Take eat,' he said, ' and be content ;
These fishes in my stead are sent
By Him who gave the tangled ram
To spare the child of Abraham.'

A beautiful portrait is the following :—

Next, the dear aunt, whose smile of cheer
And voice in dreams I see and hear,—
The sweetest woman ever Fate
Perverse denied a household mate.

      o   o   o

For well she kept her genial mood
And simple faith of maidenhood ;
Before her still a cloudland lay,
The mirage loomed across her way ;

      o   o   o

Through years of toil, and soil, and care,
From glossy tress to thin grey hair,
All unprofaned she held apart,
The virgin fancies of the heart.

The uncle who—

Innocent of books,
Was rich in lore of fields and brooks.

o   o   o

A simple, guileless, childlike man,
Content to live where life began

was Uncle Moses, "a man for the little
folks to love." He was killed in 1824 by
the fall of a tree.

The elder sister of the poet, Mary, has
her place, too, in this matchless gallery—

A full, rich nature, free to trust,
Faithful, and almost sternly just,
Keeping with many a light disguise
The secret of self-sacrifice.

and then the younger sister—

Upon the motley braided mat
Our youngest and our dearest sat,
Lifting her large, sweet, asking eyes.

The following sketch of a village schoolmaster is masterly enough to bear comparison
with Goldsmith's in "The Deserted Village":—

Brisk wielder of the birch and rule,
The master of the district school
Held at the fire his favoured place,
Its warm glow lit a laughing face
Fresh-hued and fair, where scarce appeared

The uncertain prophecy of beard.
He teased the mitten-blinded cat,
Played cross-pins on my uncle's hat,
Sang songs, and told us what befalls
In classic Dartmouth's college halls.
Born the wild Northern hills among,
From whence his yeoman father wrung
By patient toil subsistence scant,
Not competence and yet not want,
He early gained the power to pay
His cheerful, self-reliant way ;
Could doff at ease his scholar's gown
To peddle wares from town to town ;
Or through the long vacations reach
In lonely lowland districts teach,
Where all the droll experience found
At stranger hearths in boarding round,
The moonlit skater's keen delight,
The sleigh-drive through the frosty night,
The rustic party, with its rough
Accompaniment of blind-man's-buff,
And whirling plate, and forfeits paid,
His winter task a pastime made.
Happy the snow-locked homes wherein
He tuned his merry violin,
Or played the athlete in the barn,
Or held the good dame's winding-yarn
Or mirth-provoking versions told
Of classic legends rare and old,
Wherein the scenes of Greece and Rome
Had all the commonplace of home,

And little seemed at best the odds
'Twixt Yankee pedlars and old gods ;
Where Pindus-born Araxes took
The guise of any grist-mill brook,
And dread Olympus at his will
Became a huckleberry hill.

The Whittier home was the very place
in which poetical instincts might quicken, nor
were there wanting those influences which
under Divine blessing would form a high and
pure character.

"In the Whittier family," we are told,
"the reading of the Holy Scriptures was a
constant practice. On First-Day afternoon,
especially, the mother would read them with
the children, endeavouring to impress their
minds with familiar conversation ; and to this
early and habitual instruction we may attri-
bute in great measure the full and accurate
knowledge of Bible History which the poems
of J. G. Whittier indicate, as well as the strong
bias, in favour of moral reform which was so
early manifested. It is a tradition in the
family that when J. G. Whittier was very

young he often sought from his father and
others a solution of his doubts respecting the
morality of certain acts of the patriarchs and
other holy men of old ; and at one time he
declared that King David could not have been
a member of the Society of Friends, because
he was a man of war."

The visits of travelling Friends to Haviland,
too, must often have raised the thoughts of
the children to higher things than the life of
home and village. On one occasion, we are
told, no fewer than sixteen Friends were
housed for the night under John Whittier's
hospitable roof. Ministers from England were
not seldom guests, and among them came
William Forster, the father of the late Right
Hon. William Edward Forster. This visit is
alluded to in Whittier's poem beginning—

> The years are many since his hand
> Was laid upon my head,
> Too weak and young to understand
> The serious words he said.

Yet the poem is a witness of the lasting
blessing of this one incident.

In this quiet home, where ancestral evangels spoke from every wall and oaken beam, where parents and brothers and sisters lived in earthly love, and together sought the heavenly, where Christian pilgrims stayed to break bread, and Nature uttered her thousand litanies around— young Whittier was growing to the proportions of the Happy Warrior, he

> Who, when brought
> Into the tasks of real life, hath wrought
> Upon the plan that pleased his boyish thought.

CHAPTER III.

THE YOUNG IDEA.

" Still as my horizon grew,
Larger grew my riches too ;
All the world I saw or knew
Seemed a complex Chinese toy
Fashioned for a barefoot boy ! "

"THE BAREFOOT BOY."

————

" A wit in youth not over dull, heavy, knotty, and lumpish, but hard, tough, and though somewhat staffish, both for learning and the whole course of living proveth always best."

ROGER ASCHAM.

————

JOHN GREENLEAF WHITTIER'S first schoolmaster was Joshua Coffin, destined to be also his life-long friend. Coffin is not the genial pedagogue who figures in Snow-Bound, but he has his place in Whittier's verse. In the school-house, an old brown building, long since removed, we might linger, if we pleased, over Whittier's slate and spelling book, but we shall find something better worth resuscitating in a certain boyish infatuation, the story of which is enshrined in some charming verses entitled " In School-Days."

> Still sits the school-house by the road,
>   A ragged beggar sunning ;
> Around it still the sumachs grow.
>   And blackberry-vines are running.
>
> Within, the master's desk is seen,
>   Deep scarred by raps official ;
> The warping-floor, the battered seats,
>   The jack-knife's carved initial ;
>
> The charcoal frescoes on its wall ;
>   Its door's worn sill, betraying
> The feet that, creeping low to school,
>   Went storming out to playing !
>
> Long years ago a winter sun
>   Shone over it at setting ;
> Lit up its western window-panes,
>   And low eaves' icy fretting
>
> It touched the tangled golden curls,
>   And brown eyes full of grieving,
> Of one who still her steps delayed
>   When all the school were leaving.
>
> For near her stood the little boy
>   Her childish favour singled :
> His cap pulled low upon a face
>   Where pride and shame were mingled.

Pushing with restless feet the snow
　　To right and left, he lingered ;—
As restlessly her tiny hands
　　The blue-checked apron fingered.

He saw her lift her eyes ; he felt
　　The soft hand's light caressing,
And heard the tremble of her voice,
　　As if a fault confessing.

"I'm sorry that I spelt the word :
　　I hate to go above you,
Because,"—the brown eyes lower fell—
　　"Because, you see, I love you !"

Still memory to a grey-haired man
　　That sweet child-face is showing.
Dear girl ! the grasses on her grave
　　Have forty years been growing !

He lives to learn, in life's hard school,
　　How few who pass above him
Lament their triumph and his loss,
　　Like her,—because they love him.

Whittier was seven when he came under Joshua Coffin's mild rule. Of the next six or seven years what shall be said ?

A boy's will is the wind's will,
And the thoughts of youth are long, long thoughts.

Whittier's years passed as other country boys' do, and it will be needful to dwell only on a few points and incidents involved in a

true understanding of his mental development.
A free country life was his—

> I was rich in flowers and trees,
> Humming-birds and honey-bees ;
> For my sport the squirrel played,
> Plied the snouted mole his spade ;
> For my taste the blackberry cone
> Purpled over hedge and stone ;
> Laughed the brook for my delight,
> Through the day and through the night,
> Whispering at the garden wall,
> Talked with me from fall to fall ;
> Mine the sand rimmed pickerel pond,
> Mine the walnut slopes beyond,
> Mine, on bending orchard trees,
> Apples of Hesperides.
>
>   ◦   ◦   ◦
>
>   O for festal dainties spread,
> Like my bowl of milk and bread,—
> Pewter spoon and bowl of wood,
> On the door-stone, grey and rude !
> O'er me, like a regal tent,
> Cloudy-ribbed, the sunset bent,
> Purple curtained, fringed with gold,
> Looped in many a wind-swung fold ;
> While for music came the play
> Of the pied frogs' orchestra ;
> And, to light the noisy choir,
> Lit the fly his lamp of fire.
> I was monarch : pomp and joy
> Waited on the barefoot boy !

But the boy's fancy took other and more fearsome flights. Those of us who have lived, especially in boyhood, in some remote part whence superstition has not been banished by the steam-plough and the flippant bicycle, know how the uncanny element seems to be everywhere, to threaten from every copse, and waver above the forsaken beds of rushes. Such a district was the valley of the Merrimac when Whittier was a boy, and many a tale of these signs and wonders is to be found in his prose writings. One of his earliest recollections was of an old woman, living about two miles from the homestead, who was believed to be a witch, and at last, to get rid of her tormentors, went before a Justice of the Peace to make oath that she was a Christian woman, and no witch. Of course there were a number of well-established ghosts, including a headless one, who was seen at times walking under the riverside willows carrying his head in a tin pail. There was a mill that worked by no earthly agency, and a midnight cry from the ground,

and stories of human beings fascinated by
rattle-snakes. In such poems as the "Witch
of Wenham," the "Witch's Daughter," "The
Rattlesnake Hunter," "The Old Burial Ground,"
and many others, we catch glimpses of these
village terrors. Whittier loved to stir them
up and play with them.

From the graves of old traditions I part the black-
berry vines,
Wipe the moss from off the head-stones, and retouch
the faded lines.

Another set of impressions came from the
visits of gypsies, pedlars, and such wandering
folk. Whittier's description of them is a
capital piece of poet's prose. "The advent
of wandering beggars or 'old stragglers' was
an event of no ordinary interest in the
monotonous quietude of our farm-life. They
had their periodical revolutions and transits;
we could calculate them like eclipses or new
moons. Some were sturdy knaves, fat and
saucy, and whenever they ascertained that the
'men folks' were absent, would order pro-

visions and cider like men who expected to
pay for them, seating themselves at the hearth
or table with the air of Falstaff—'Shall I not
take mine ease in mine inn?' Others, poor,
pale, patient, like Sterne's monk, came creep-
ing up to the door, hat in hand, standing there
in their grey wretchedness with a look of heart-
break and forlornness which was never without
its effect on our juvenile sensibilities. At times,
however, we experienced a slight revulsion of
feeling when even these humblest children
of sorrow somewhat petulantly rejected our
proffered bread and cheese, and demanded
instead a glass of cider. Whatever the temperance society might in such cases have done,
it was not in our hearts to refuse the poor
creatures a draught of their favourite beverage ;
and wasn't it a satisfaction to see their sad,
melancholy faces light up as we handed them
the full pitcher, and, on receiving it back
empty from their brown wrinkled hands, to
hear them, half breathless from their long, delicious draught, thanking us for the favour as

'dear, good children!' Not unfrequently these
wandering tests of our benevolence made their
appearance in interesting groups of man, woman,
and child, picturesque in their squalidness, and
manifesting a maudlin affection which would
have done honour to the revellers at Poosie-
Nansie's, immortal in the cantata of Burns.
I remember some who were the victims of
monomania—haunted and hunted by some dark
thought—possessed by a fixed idea. One, a
black eyed, wild-haired woman, with a whole
tragedy of sin, shame, and suffering written in
her countenance, used often to visit us, warm herself by our winter fire, and supply herself with a
stock of cakes and cold meat ; but was never
known to answer a question or to ask one. She
never smiled ; the cold, stony look of her eye
never changed ; a silent, impassive face, frozen
rigid by some great wrong or sin. We used
to look with awe upon the " still woman,"
and think of the demoniac of Scripture who
had a " dumb spirit." One—I think I see
him now, grim, quaint, and ghastly, working

his slow way up to our door—used to gather
herbs by the wayside and call himself doctor.
He was bearded like a he goat and used to
counterfeit lameness, yet when he supposed
himself alone, would travel on lustily as if
walking for a wager. At length, as if in
punishment of his deceit, he met with an
accident in his rambles and became lame in
earnest, hobbling ever after with difficulty on
his gnarled crutches. Another used to go
stooping, like Bunyan's pilgrim, under a pack
made of an old bed-sacking, stuffed out into
most plethoric dimensions, tottering on a pair
of small, meagre legs, and peering out with
his wild hairy face from under his burden
like a big-bodied spider. That 'man with
the pack.' always inspired me with awe and
reverence. Huge, almost sublime in its tense
rotundity, the father of all packs, never laid
aside and never opened, what might there not
be within it? With what flesh-creeping curiosity I used to walk round about it at a safe
distance, half expecting to see its striped cover-

ing stirred by the motions of a mysterious life, or that some evil monster would leap out of it, like robbers from Ali Baba's jars, or armed men from the Trojan horse!"

What figures these! equal to any of Rembrandt's beggar kings! One more portrait must be added; "Twice a year, usually in the spring or autumn, we were honoured with a call from Jonathan Plummer, maker of verses, peddler and poet, physician and parson,—a Yankee troubadour,—first and last minstrel of the valley of the Merrimac, encircled, to my wondering young eyes, with the very nimbus of immortality. He brought with him pins, needles, tape, and cotton thread for my mother; jack-knives, razors, and soap for my father; and verses of his own composing, coarsely printed and illustrated with rude woodcuts, for the delectation of the younger branches of the family. No love-sick youth could drown himself, no deserted maiden bewail the moon, no rogue mount the gallows, without fitting Memorial in Plummer's verses. Earthquakes, fires, fevers,

and shipwrecks he regarded as personal favours
from Providence furnishing the raw material
of song or ballad. Welcome to us in our
country seclusion as Autolycus to the clown
in the 'Winter's Tale,' we listened with infinite
satisfaction to his readings of his own verses,
or to his ready improvisation upon some domestic
incident or topic suggested by his auditors.
When once fairly over the difficulties at the
outset of a new subject, his rhymes flowed
freely, 'as if he had eaten ballads, and all
men's ears grew to his tunes.' His productions
answered, as nearly as I can remember, to
Shakespeare's description of a proper ballad—
'doleful matter merrily set down, or a pleasant
theme sung lamentably.' He was scrupulously
conscientious, devout, inclined to theological
disquisitions, and withal mighty in Scripture.
He was thoroughly independent; flattered nobody, cared for nobody, trusted nobody. When
invited to sit down at our dinner table he
invariably took the precaution to place his
basket of valuables between his legs for safe

keeping. 'Never mind thy basket, Jonathan,' said my father, 'We shan't steal thy verses,' 'I'm not so sure of that,' returned the suspicious guest. 'It is written, "Trust ye not in any brother."'"

Plummer's literary talk could not have been unwelcome in a house where the almanac, the village weekly paper, and "scarce a score of books and pamphlets" were to be found, among them, let us pause to note,—

> One harmless novel, mostly hid
> From younger eyes, a book forbid,
> And poetry (or good or bad,
> A single book was all we had),
> Where Ellwood's meek, drab-skirted Muse,
>   A stranger to the heathen Nine,
>   Sang with a somewhat nasal whine,
> The wars of David and the Jews.

But one day Joshua Coffin came in bringing a copy of Burns, and about the same time a "pawky auld carle" of a wandering Scotchman turned up, and after eating his bread and cheese and drinking his mug of cider, he sang "Bonnie Doon," "Highland Mary," and

"Auld Lang Syne," with spirit, and in a full
rich voice. The boy's heart was in a tumult;
and trivial as was the occasion, it was great
in result. He threw himself into Burns's
poetry with boyish rapture, first taking
pains to master the glossary. "It was about
the first poetry I had ever read (with the
exception of that of the Bible of which I had
been a close student), and it had a lasting
influence upon me. I began to make rhymes
myself, and to imagine stories and adventures."
"I found," he adds, "that the things out of
which poems came were not, as I had always
imagined, somewhere away off in a world and
life lying outside the edge of our own New
Hampshire sky,—they were right here about
my feet and among the people I knew. The
common things of life, I found, were full of
poetry."

The boy's mind was now set toward
the Muse. Looking on Nature with enlarged
eyes he felt that it was in him to re-create
her loveliness in words rhythmic as the Merrimac,

soft and wooing as Kenoza's dream, or awful as the voices of the pines on Ramoth Hill; and with these there perhaps mingled harsher notes, vague suggestions as of—

Ancestral voices, prophesying war.

More than one poem has been indicated by different writers as Whittier's first effort. From an American biography, just published, by W. S. Kennedy, a gentleman who seems to be deeply versed in Whittier lore, it would appear that we have no earlier lines of the poet's than eight stanzas on "William Penn," written at the age of sixteen. These lines are surprisingly strong considering the circumstances of their production. Three of the verses are as follows:

Founder of Pennsylvania! Thou
　　Didst feel it, when thy words of peace
　　Smoothed the stern chieftain's swarthy brow,
　　And bade the dreadful war-dance cease.

On Schuylkill's banks no fortress frowned,
　　The peaceful cot alone was there;
No beacon fires the hill-tops crowned,
　　No Death-shot swept the Delaware.

> In manners meek, in precepts mild,
>   Thou and thy friends serenely taught
> The savage huntsman, fierce and wild,
>   To raise to heaven his erring thought.

We are more concerned, however, with Whittier's first *published* poem, the identity of which is beyond doubt. It was entitled "The Deity," and was written when Whittier was nineteen; strange to say its appearance in the poetical corner of the Newburyport "Free Press" was wholly unlooked for by the author. His elder sister Mary, who seems to have understood her brother, and to have taken a pride in his abilities, had sent off the verses to that journal, and the first knowledge that Whittier had of it was the postman's handing him the paper containing his piece while he was mending a stone fence.

A few days after, when hoeing in a cornfield, Whittier was summoned by messenger to the house to see a stranger who desired to speak with him. This was no other than William Lloyd Garrison, who was only three years

Whittier's senior, and the editor of the "Free Press." Struck with the merit of Whittier's poem, and learning that it was the work of a mere lad, he had been sufficiently interested to drive over and seek out the would-be poet. The youth was overwhelmed with confusion and secret pride when Garrison not only spoke words of encouragement to him, but immediately began to enforce on his father the desirability of giving his son a school training. The elder Whittier, however, remonstrated with Garrison for "putting notions in the boy's head," and it would appear that he had not, as a fact, the means for carrying out Garrison's suggestions. But the Whittier household had been deeply impressed, for young Garrison's delivery of his sentiments was such as to carry conviction. It is not surprising to learn that in the same year all difficulties were overcome, and the lad left his home for Haviland Academy, only returning to his father's roof at the week-ends. Here Whittier studied in the ordinary grooves. It is said that when he

handed to his master his first composition in
prose, that gentleman could hardly be per-
suaded that it was the unaided effort of his
pupil, but became fully convinced as, week
by week, Whittier sent essays of equal or
superior merit.

Whittier's grit at this time is shown in
the fact that at the end of this first six months'
schooling he had not exceeded by a cent his
estimated expenses, still retaining the quarter
dollar which had been his surplus at the
beginning.

He lodged with the family of Mr. Abijah
Wyman Thayer, the editor and publisher of
the "Haverhill Gazette," and enjoyed the use
of his library, where he often became so ab-
sorbed in the books he found there as to be
insensible to the noise of the children playing
around him. He had a good friend, too, in
Dr. Elias Weld, who also allowed him the run
of his books. Whittier wrote of him, "He was
the one cultivated man of the neighbourhood,"
and it is he who is referred to in the passage

in " Snow Bound "—

> The wise old Doctor went his round,
> Just pausing at our door to say,
> In the brief autocratic way
> Of one who, prompt at Duty's call,
> Was free to urge her claim on all,
>   That some poor neighbour sick abed
> At night our mother's aid would need.
> For, one in generous thought and deed,
>   What mattered in the sufferer's sight
>   The Quaker matron's inward light
> The Doctor's mail of Calvin's creed?
> All hearts confess the saints elect
>   Who, twain in faith, in love agree,
> And melt not in an acid sect
>   The Christian pearl of charity!

The following interesting account of Whittier at this period is extracted from a letter addressed by Mrs. Harriet M. Pitman, of Somerville, Mass., to Francis H. Underwood, in whose biography of Whittier it appears;—" He went to school awhile at Haverhill Academy. There were pupils of all ages, from ten to twenty-five. My brother, George Minot, then about ten years old, used to say that Whittier was the best of all the big fellows, and he was

in the habit of calling him 'Uncle Toby.'
Whittier was always kind to children, and
under a very grave and quiet exterior there
was a real love of fun, and a keen sense of
the ludicrous. In society he was embarrassed,
and his manners were in consequence
sometimes brusque and cold. With intimate
friends he talked a great deal, and in a won-
derfully interesting manner; usually earnest,
often analytical, and frequently playful. He
had a great deal of wit. It was a family
characteristic. The study of human nature
was very interesting to him, and his insight
was keen. He liked to draw out his young
friends, and to suggest puzzling doubts and
queries. . . . One could never flatter him.
I never tried, but I have seen people attempt
it, and it was a signal failure. He did not
flatter, but told very wholesome and unpalatable
truths, yet in a way to spare one's self-love
by admitting of a doubt whether he was in
jest or earnest. . . . He had a retentive
memory and a marvellous store of information

on many subjects. I once saw a little commonplace book of his,—full of quaint things, and
as interesting as Southey's."

A schoolfellow, since become a minister,
has thus written of Whittier as he remembers
him at Haviland :—

"I remember him as a big boy whom we
were all proud to know, and by whom we all
esteemed it the greatest of honours to be noticed.
Many and many a time I remember seeing his
slate going about from hand to hand with some
little poem that he had struck off in school.
I used always to deem it an exquisite pleasure,
as well as a deep honour if the slate were
passed to me. I do not remember if Mr. Whittier
ever approved of this proceeding on the part
of his schoolmates. He was always modest in
showing his productions, and when his slate
was passed on from hand to hand, as I have
told you, it was generally the result of some
breach of confidence on the part of some one
of his particular friends who sat near him.
These verses were often of a humorous nature,

and often had as subjects things to be found in the schoolroom. Many, however, were of a more serious and thoughtful character."

Whittier taught for a while at West Amesbury and then returned to the Academy for another six months' study. In the autumn of 1828 he left, and through the good offices of his old friend Garrison, was invited to Boston to write for the "American Manufacturer." In June, 1829, he returned home, his services being needed on the farm, and there remained for the next year. But he did not drop his pen. In the first half of the year 1830 he edited the Haverhill "Gazette" in his leisure, and at this time he was contributing articles and poems to a more important paper, the "New England Review" of Hartford, Connecticut, edited by George D. Prentice. Much to his surprise he was soon afterwards asked to edit this paper while Mr. Prentice was away in Kentucky. "I could not have been more utterly astonished," said Whittier, "if I had been told that I had been appointed prime minister to the great Khan of Tartary."

The directors of the paper, on seeing Whittier, were much surprised at his youth. "But," says a biographer, "he discreetly kept silence, letting them do most of the talking. Here most assuredly his Quaker doctrine of silence stood him in good stead; since, if we may believe him, he was most wofully deficient in a knowledge of the intricacies of the political situation of the time."

We see by the following extract, taken from the "New England Review" in 1829 (before his appointment to the editorship) that Whittier had laid the foundations of his fame before his twenty-second year.

J. G. WHITTIER.

"'The culmination of that man's fame will be a proud period in the history of our literature.' This generous tribute to the abilities of our friend Whittier was contained in a letter which we recently received from one of the most distinguished men in the country. The tribute was merited. . . . . Whittier is a poet and a Christian."

Whittier is now fairly launched in literary
life, with the responsibilities of manhood des-
cending on him ; this chapter therefore may fitly
close with part of a poem written in 1830, the
year of his appointment as Editor of the Hartford paper. This piece, entitled "The Quaker-
ess," was suppressed by the poet with others
which his riper judgment condemned, but the
lines quoted have a reflected biographical interest that seems to warrant their introduction
here.

                              Unadorned,
    Save by her youthful charms, and with a garb
    Simple as Nature's self, why turn to her
    The proud and gifted, and the versed in all
    The pageantry of fashion ?
                              She hath not
    Moved down the dance to music, when the hall
    Is lighted up like sunshine, and the thrill
    Of the light viol and the mellow flute,
    And the deep tones of manhood, softened down
    To very music, melt upon the ear.
    She has not mingled with the hollow world
    Nor tampered with its mockeries, until all
    The delicate perceptions of the heart,
    The innate modesty, the watchful sense
    Of maiden dignity, are lost within
    The maze of fashion and the din of crowds.

In the chastened beauty of that eye,
And in the beautiful play of that red lip,
And in the quiet smile, and in the voice
Sweet as the tuneful greeting of a bird
To the first flowers of spring-time, there is more
Than the perfection of the painter's skill
Or statuary's moulding. *Mind* is there,
The pure and lofty attributes of soul.
The seal of virtue, the exceeding grace
Of meekness blended with a maiden pride ;
Nor deem ye that beneath the gentle smile,
And the calm temper of a chastened mind
No warmth of passion kindles, and no tide
Of quick and earnest feeling courses on
From the warm heart's pulsations.

                  There are springs
Of deep and pure affection, hidden now
Within that quiet bosom, which but wait
The thrilling of some kindly touch, to flow
Like waters from the Desert-rock of old.

CHAPTER IV.

THE DEW OF YOUTH.

"I wait and watch ; before my eyes
  Methinks the night grows thin and grey ;
I wait and watch the eastern skies
To see the golden spears uprise
  Beneath the oriflamme of day !

*   *   *

O power to do ! O baffled will !
  O prayer and action ! ye are one
Who may not strive may yet fulfil
  The harder task of standing still,
And good but wished with God is done."

"WAITING."

"In every well-conditioned stripling, as I conjecture, there already blooms a certain prospective paradise, cheered by some fairest Eve. Perhaps the whole is but the lovelier, if Cherubim and the Flaming Sword divide it from all footsteps of men ; and grant him, the imaginative stripling, only the view, not the entrance. . . . . "

CARLYLE.

AMERICAN poetry and American journalism were young in 1830 ; but the first was distinguished by the feebleness and the second by the roughness of juvenility. Whittier, as a candidate for honours in both, occupied the position of nearly every young American poet both then and since ; and we can see how this doubling of parts was adding to the strength and versatility of his intellect in these eighteen months at Hartford before he received his call to

> A strife so long,
> That, ere it closed, the black abundant hair,
> Of boyhood rested silver-sown and spare
> On Manhood's temples.

Whittier's qualifications for the editorship of the " New England Weekly Review " were, as we have said, at least doubtful ; he himself appears to have considered his knowledge of public affairs inadequate, but not caring to lose the opportunity, he boldly went forward, and accepted the post.

George Prentice bade farewell to his readers in the issue of the paper dated July 5, 1830, and wrote,—

" Mr. J. G. Whittier, an old favourite with the public, will probably have charge of the

Review in my absence, and I cannot do less than congratulate my readers on the prospect of their more familiar acquaintance with a gentleman of such powerful energies, and such exalted purity and sweetness of character. I have made some enemies among those whose good opinion I value, but no rational man can ever be the enemy of Mr. Whittier."

Files of the "New England Weekly Review" are not to be found at the British Museum; if they were they might afford interesting matter for comment. It is said that under Whittier's editorship the paper, as we might confidently expect, was free from the personalities then carried to such extremes in American newspapers. Whittier's contributions, other than editorials, included more than forty poems and a large number of sketches and tales in prose. These poems were ruthlessly suppressed by Whittier in later life, with three exceptions. The "Vaudois Teacher" is included in all editions; after translation into French it became a favourite among the Waldenses, who, for many years, supposed it to be the work of a French author; but when they learned its true origin they sent a grateful address to Whittier. "The Star of Bethlehem" and "The Frost Spirit" have also passed into the permanent collections of Whittier's verse.

Some of these sketches and poems, with others not contributed to the Review, were published in 1831 in a thin duodecimo volume, and this was Whittier's first book. Both prose and poetry are indifferent, but the legends preserved are valuable for their own sake; one of them is of a spectre ship, said to have sailed on her last fateful voyage from Salem with a pair of lovers on board.

At this time Whittier gave further evidence of his interest in the legendary lore of "New England" by writing an introduction to the "Remains" of his friend J. G. C. Brainard. Brainard died young, and, with him, the promise of a poet. Whittier edited his poems as a friend anxious to commend them to the world, yet his desire to be an

honest critic is very apparent. The introduction is interesting as a specimen of Whittier's
style, and as showing the extent of his reading
which was more than ordinarily wide. In
thirty-six pages Whittier gives proof of his
acquaintance with Locke, Newton, Akenside,
Blackstone, Byron, Keats, Shelley, Wordsworth,
Coleridge, Goethe, and other authors. The
following passage is interesting—

"It has often been said that the New
World is deficient in the elements of poetry
and romance ; that its bards must of necessity
linger over the classic ruins of other lands ;
and draw their sketches of character from
foreign sources, and paint Nature under the
soft beauty of an Eastern sky. On the con-
trary, New England is full of Romance ; and
her writers would do well to follow the example of Brainard. The great forest which
our fathers penetrated — the red men — their
struggle and their disappearance—the Powwow
and the war-dance—the savage inroad and the
English sally—the tale of superstition and the

scenes of witchcraft—all these are rich ma-
terials of poetry. We have indeed no classic
vale of Tempe—no haunted Parnassus—no
temple, grey with years, and hallowed by the
gorgeous pageantry of idol worship—no towers
and castles over whose moonlit ruins gathers
the green pall of the ivy. But we have mountains pillaring a sky as blue as that which
bends over classic Olympus; streams as bright
and beautiful as those of Greece and Italy,
and forests richer and nobler than those which
of old were haunted by Sylph and Dryad."

In March, 1831, Whittier went to see the old
folks at Haverhill. The journey from Hartford
was a long and fatiguing one, and at the end of it
he wrote in a strain of lively self-banter—"I
have had a shocking time of it, and ever since
have dreamed of stages upset, of ten-feet snow-
drifts, and mud immeasurable and interminable.
Every bone in my body aches at the bare idea
of my journey. I would as soon ride bare-
backed the Rozinante of Don Quixote. . . .
A conveyance in that rascally French diligence

which Sterne complains of would be a luxury to it; and I can easily imagine how poor Sancho Panza must have suffered while tossed in the blanket by the muleteers at the enchanted inn. When I left Hartford I was neither more nor less than a disciple of Penn and Ellwood, but before I reached the end of my journey I was to all intents and purposes a shaking Quaker."

In the same letter, quoted by Mr. Underwood, Whittier writes :—" And where, you will ask, are my sentimentalisms and love adventures? Alas, my dear fellow, these are not the days of romance. . . . But I *can* say that I have clasped more than one fair hand, and read my welcome in more than one bright eye since my arrival."

Here it seems appropriate to say the little that is to be said about Whittier's love-story, as it may be conveniently called.

Only a few golden threads straying through his poetry betray what of romance there was in his life, or hint at what might have been. It would have been natural to suppose that a young man, early conspicuous by his ability and graces of character, would have found one with whom to

> Walk this world
> Yoked in all exercise of noble thought.

But such was not the case, and to the end of his long life Whittier remained single. The causes of this are not for us to explore, yet it would be as improper for the biographer to make no use of the clues which the poet has himself given to the secret, as it would be to push conjecture beyond the veil he has dropped.

From an early age Whittier's qualities of heart and head made him a favourite with the opposite sex. When at Haverhill Academy "the gatherings of young people," says one, who remembers him there, " were never thought complete without Whittier ; and the young ladies of the school and village were never quite so happy as when they were invited to meet him at a tea-party."

We can therefore understand the warmth

of his greeting on all hands when he again
set foot in Haverhill in 1831, a handsome
young man of twenty-three, and famous already
for several hundred miles round. Possibly it
was out of the social events of this visit
that there arose the feelings which prompted
him to write, a few months later, a poem,
entitled, " Isabel."

I do not love thee, Isabel, and yet thou art most
    fair,
I know the tempting of thy lips, the witchcraft of
    thy hair,
The winsome smile that might beguile the shy bird
    from his tree,
But from their spell I know so well, I shake my
    manhood free.

I might have loved thee, Isabel; I know I should
    if aught
Of all thy words and ways had told of one unselfish
    thought ;
If through the cloud of fashion, the pictured veil of
    art,
One casual flash had broken warm, earnest from the
    heart.

But words are idle, Isabel, and if I praise or blame,
Or cheer or warn, it matters not ; thy life will be
    the same ;

Still free to use, and still abuse, unmindful of the
    harm,
The fatal gift of beauty, the power to choose and
    charm.

Then go thy way, fair Isabel, nor heed that from thy
    train
A doubtful follower falls away, enough will still
    remain.
But what the long-rebuking years may bring to them
    or thee,
No prophet and no prophet's son am I to guess or
    see.

I do not love thee, Isabel ; I would as soon put on
A crown of slender frost-work beneath the heated sun,
Or chase the winds of summer, or trust the sleeping
    sea,
Or lean upon a shadow as think of loving thee.

Here we seem to listen to the expression
of a youthful disenchantment soon to be for-
gotten, but the lines show the moral earnest-
ness Whittier carried into his love-making.

It is in a poem written several years later
that nearly all students of Whittier's poetry are
agreed to find the veiled tragedy, if tragedy
it were, of the poet's life. The poem is entitled, "Memories," and is quoted entire :—

MEMORIES.

A beautiful and happy girl,
  With step as light as summer air,
Eyes glad with smiles, and brow of pearl,
Shadowed by many a careless curl
  Of unconfined and flowing hair ;
A seeming child in everything,
  Save thoughtful brow and ripening charms,
As Nature wears the smile of Spring
  When sinking into summer's arms.

A mind rejoicing in the light
  Which melted through its graceful bower,
Leaf after leaf, dew-moist and bright,
And stainless in its holy white,
  Unfolding like a morning flower :
A heart, which, like a fine-toned lute,
  With every breath of feeling woke,
And, even when the tongue was mute,
  From eye and lip in music spoke.

How thrills once more the lengthening chain
  Of memory, at the thought of thee !
Old hopes, which long in dust have lain,
Old dreams, come thronging back again,
  And boyhood lives again in me ;
I feel its glow upon my cheek,
  Its fulness of the heart is mine,
As when I learned to hear thee speak,
  Or raised my doubtful eye to thine.

I hear again thy low replies,
  I feel thy arm within my own,
And timidly again uprise
The fringèd lids of hazel eyes,
  With soft brown tresses overblown.
Ah! memories of sweet summer eves,
  Of moonlit wave and willowy way,
Of stars and flowers, and dewy leaves,
  And smiles and tones more dear than they!

Ere this, thy quiet eye hath smiled
  My picture of thy youth to see,
When, half a woman, half a child
Thy very artlessness beguiled,
  And folly's self seemed wise in thee ;
I too can smile, when o'er that hour
  The lights of memories backward stream,
Yet feel the while that manhood's power
  Is vainer than my boyhood's dream.

Years have passed on, and left their trace
  Of graver care and deeper thought ;
And unto me the calm, cold face
Of manhood, and to thee the grace
  Of woman's pensive beauty brought.
More wide, perchance, for blame than praise,
  The School-boys humble name has flown ;
Thine, in the green and quiet ways
  Of unobtrusive goodness known.

And wider yet in thought and deed
  Diverge our pathways, one in youth ;

Thine the Genevan's sternest creed,
While answers to my spirit's need
 The Derby dalesman's simple truth.
For thee, the priestly rite and prayer,
 And holy day, and solemn psalm ;
For me, the silent reverence where
 My brethren gather, slow and calm.

Yet hath thy spirit left on me
 An impress Time has worn not out,
And something of myself in thee,
A shadow from the past, I see,
 Lingering, even yet, thy way about ;
Not wholly can the heart unlearn
 That lesson of its better hours,
Nor yet has Time's dull footstep worn
 To common dust that path of flowers.

Thus while at times before our eyes
 The shadows melt, and fall apart,
And, smiling through them, round us lies
The warm light of our morning skies,—
 The Indian Summer of the heart !—
In secret sympathies of mind,
 In founts of feeling which retain
Their pure, fresh flow, we yet may find
 Our early dreams not wholly vain !

The full depth of meaning in this beautiful poem is not for us, yet, once known, the
"brown tresses" of the New England maiden

haunt our thoughts of Whittier, like the golden hair of Alice Winn flashing across Elia's melancholy page.

Even more enigmatical is the poem entitled "The Henchman," written by the poet in his seventieth year. Any disposition to regard this effusion as a mere idle imitation of mediæval poesy is defeated by its suppressed fervour and by its concentration and finish, rivalling some choice Elizabethan lyric; while coming from a poet who had left fifty years behind him the dubious culte of "art for art's sake," it can scarcely have had other source than some old well-spring of love. Further we dare not inquire; "the heart knoweth its own bitterness, neither doth the stranger intermeddle therewith."

THE HENCHMAN.

My lady walks her morning round,
My lady's page her fleet greyhound,
My lady's hair the fond winds stir,
And all the bird's make songs for her.

Her thrushes sing in Rathburn bowers,
And Rathburn side is gay with flowers;

But ne'er like hers, in flower or bird,
Was beauty seen or music heard.

The distance of the stars is hers;
The least of all her worshippers,
The dust beneath her dainty heel,
She knows not that I see or feel.

O proud and calm!—she cannot know
Where'er she goes with her I go,
O cold and fair!—she cannot guess
I kneel to share her hound's caress!

Gay knights beside her hunt and hawk,
I rob their ears of her sweet talk;
Her suitors come from east and west,
I steal her smiles from every guest.

Unheard of her, in loving words,
I greet her with the song of birds;
I reach her with her green-armed bowers,
I kiss her with the lips of flowers.

The hound and I are on her trail,
The wind and I uplift her veil;
As if the calm cold moon she were,
And I the tide, I follow her.

As unrebuked as they, I share
The licence of the sun and air,
And in a common homage hide
My worship from her scorn and pride.

World-wide apart, and yet so near,
I breathe her charmèd atmosphere,

Wherein to her my service brings
The reverence due to holy things.

Her maiden pride, her haughty name,
My dumb devotion shall not shame;
The love that no return doth crave
To knightly levels lifts the slave.

No lance have I, in joust or fight,
To splinter in my lady's sight;
But, at her feet, how blest were I
For any need of hers to die.

This poem, whatever its inspiration, must be numbered among those by which posterity will appraise the genius of the "Quaker Poet."

Whittier's stay at Haverhill was prolonged owing to the illness of his father, who passed away in July, 1831. The poet was obliged to return to his active duties at Hartford, leaving his mother and sisters, for the present, to lament his cheery presence at the old fireside with its vacant chair.

But he was soon with them again. His health had never been equal to his conscientious diligence, and he must often have sighed to put his brains to higher work than newspaper writing, in which the hurry, inseparable from journalism, defeated all ambition to reason justly and to write with elegance.

The following glowing lines, written at this time, reveal the young poet's aspirations.

Land of my fathers! if the name,
   Now humble and unwed to fame,
     Hereafter burn upon the lip
As one of those which may not die,
     Linked in eternal fellowship,
With visions pure, and strong, and high—
If the wild dreams which quicken now
The throbbing pulse of heart and brow,
Hereafter take a real form,
Like spectres changed to beings warm,
   And over temples warm and gray
The star-like crown of glory shine,
     Thine be the bard's undying lay,
The murmur of his praise be thine!

One does not criticise such lines. Nor can they be understood but by recalling our "volcanic" days, when our own secret imaginings were of future fame and applause, and the spirit, unyoked as yet to actual and possible tasks, wandered, fancy free, into the favours and honours of tho world.

CHAPTER V.

THROUGH THE FIRE.

" God said : ' Break thou these yokes ; undo
  These heavy burdens.   I ordain
A work to last thy whole life through,
A ministry of strife and pain.'

Forego thy dreams of lettered ease,
  Put thou the scholar's promise by,
The rights of man are more than these,
  He heard, and answered : ' Here am I !' "
                                        " SUMNER."

———

" The way of life is wonderful; it is by abandonment."
                                        EMERSON.

WHITTIER had never lost sight of his old friend and helper, William Lloyd Garrison.   That young soldier of journalism, after leaving the Newburyport " Free Press," had gone to Boston, where he was soon engaged in editing a temperance paper.   While in this city he met Benjamin Lundy, a Baltimore Friend and pioneer of Abolitionism, whose Anti-Slavery journal, " The Genius of Universal

Emancipation," had been, since 1812, the weak and solitary voice raised in the press against the Slave evil; even it pleaded only for the gradual extinction of the system.

Benjamin Lundy, a Quaker of the "old Foxian orgasm," had come into New England to try to enlist the clergy in the cause he held sacred, but failing to do so, his disappointment was bitter. In this situation he stumbled on young Garrison. His words were not lost here, and two years later, in 1831, Garrison joined him in the management of the paper.

Let us interrupt our narrative with a question, and its answer. What, briefly, was the pedigree of the Anti-Slavery movement? Something as follows :—

In 1620 two ships lowered their sails in American rivers ; the pilgrim fathers were aboard one ; the other disgorged a score of African slaves. Thus at the very beginning were the tares sown with the wheat. From that time till the Declaration of Independence,

the importation of slaves went on, encouraged
by England, until 300,000 black men had made
the voyage from Africa to the States, from
liberty to chains.

Prudential considerations at length began to
suggest that some limits should be set to these
numbers, and several States imposed taxes on
slave-importations, while Massachussetts endeav-
oured, in 1771, to abolish the trade entirely
within her borders. But all these acts were
persistently thwarted by England, and the evil
flourished until its roots had struck deep into
the national life.

Very early did the voice of the Society
of Friends pierce public apathy with its protest
against " the wild and guilty fantasy that man
can hold property in man." John Woolman,
Anthony Benezet, Elias Hicks, Benjamin Lundy,
Levi Coffin, and many others, were the Society's
spokesmen and henchmen in the cause. Then
came with the growth of moral sentiment
the formation of Anti-slavery Societies, of
which several were started in the last decade

of the 18th century. We hear, too, the voices of statesmen rising on the side of Abolition. Jefferson foresaw the inevitable conflict between right and wrong; "I tremble for my country," he cried, "when I remember that God is just." In 1787 we find free and slave states distinguished by Congress. In 1831 Nat Turner's conspiracy and the massacre of sixty whites brought slavery to the front in the Virginia Legislature and remarkable utterances were heard. Said one member, "I thank God that the spell is broken, and that we now, for the first time, can say what we think. If slavery can be eradicated, in God's name let us put an end to it."

These were but rumblings of the approaching storm. The masses shrank to the last from the giant problem; it was found that wholesale releases of slaves were dangerous to order, and many believed that Abolition would upset commercial economy. In the South, especially, men's ears were "stuffed with cotton" against the rising cry for Abo-

lition. Thus a policy of *laissez faire* ruled
when Garrison listened to Benjamin Lundy's
earnest, almost prayerful, words in Boston.

William Lloyd Garrison was a great man
in waiting. Friend and foe alike were to
feel his unsuspected might. " One of God's
nobility," Harriet Martineau called him,
" covered all over with the stars and orders
of the spiritual realm." He assailed fearfully,
and was unassailable.

When Garrison put his hand to Benjamin Lundy's paper it was to reconstruct it.
There must be no temporising, no fractional
work. " Unconditional emancipation is the
immediate duty of the master, and the immediate right of the slave." This word went
through America ; Garrison meanwhile lying
in prison for it. On his speedy release,
to which Whittier contributed, the intrepid
journalist decided to go to Boston. Here he
immediately founded the " Liberator." A
truly earth-shaking trumpet blast was now
sounded across the roofs of Boston, to be

carried on every wind to a nation's ear.
" I am aware that many object to the
severity of my language, but is there not
cause for severity ?   I will be as harsh as
truth, and as uncompromising as justice. On
this subject I do not wish to think, or
speak, or write with moderation. No ! No !
Tell a man whose house is on fire to give
a moderate alarm ; tell the mother to gradually
extricate her babe from the fire into which
it has fallen ; but urge me not to use moderation in a cause like the present. *I am
in earnest—I will not equivocate—I will not
excuse—I will not retreat a single inch—and
I will be heard.*"

" The whole land," we are told, " was
speedily filled with excitement, the apathy
of years was broken, and the new dispensa-
tion of immediatism was justified by results."

Yet these thunderbolts were hurled from
a hole of an office, where Garrison alternately
wielded the pen and composing stick, assisted
by one man, Isaac Knapp of Newburyport,

and a negro boy. Lowell's picture is touching.

> In a small chamber, friendless and unseen,
>   Toiled o'er his type, one poor unlearned man,
> The place was dark, unfurnitured and mean,
>   Yet there the freedom of a race began.

> O Truth! O freedom! low are ye still born,
>   In the rude stable, in the manger nursed;
> What humble hands unbar these gates of morn,
>   Through which the splendour of the new day
>   burst.

> O small beginnings, ye are great and strong,
>   Based on a faithful heart and a weariless brain,
> Ye build the future fair, ye conquer wrong,
>   Ye earn the crown, and wear it not in vain.

Here, then, was something to greaten life for young spirits—the inception of a glorious cause, and a challenge to the friends of freedom and justice to present themselves in the light of the sun for warfare, and always warfare, until this hoary wrong should be done away.

Whittier was at Haverhill. He was comforting his bereaved mother and sisters, and working hard with his pen, now enlisted in the service of Buckingham's "New England Magazine" of Boston.

Already he had thought much on the slave question, and indeed, had made a close study of its historical and ethical aspects. Yet his interest in it was clearly somewhat academical. He was in fact settling to the idea of a life of congenial literary work and large leisure. Garrison all the while saw this from his stronghold, and grieved. In a letter he wrote in 1833 to three Haverhill young ladies, he approached them on the point :—" You excite my curiosity and interest by informing me that my dearly-beloved Whittier is a *friend* and townsman of yours. Can we not induce him to devote his brilliant genius more to the advancement of our cause, and kindred enterprises, and less to the creations of romance and fancy, and the disturbing incidents of political life ? "

Whittier, on his part, had watched Garrison's brave doings with generous admiration. Little by little, something was taking hold of his heart. As month by month the comparative leisure of his home-life was invaded by the sounds of a vast movement among men, the young poet's soul was stirred greatly within him. At last came a call that he dared not disobey — to the baptism wherewith he was to be baptised, and to the mission that he was ordained to accomplish. In 1833 he published, at his own expense, his "Justice and Expediency," and this was the determining act of his life.

The pamphlet was a scathing one, and the fire that glows in every line is the fire that is soon to break forth in the "Songs of Liberty." It was thus that he rebuked those who urged that New England, having no part in the slave system, was without responsibility.

"Why are we thus willing to believe a lie? New England not responsible! Bound by the United States constitution to protect the slave holder in his sins, and yet not responsible! Palliating the evil, hiding the evil,

voting for the evil, do we not participate
in it ? Members of one confederacy, children
of one family, the curse and the shame, this
sin against our brother, and the sin against
our God,—all the iniquity of slavery which is
revealed to man, and all which crieth in the
ear, or is manifested in the eye of Jehovah,
will assuredly be visited upon all our people."

It is not within the scope of this little
book to follow the progress of the Anti-Slavery
Cause in the States during the next twenty
years. It was withstood in Congress, in the
street, in the press ; it was delayed by dissensions within ; it was resisted by mobs,
and in the end by armies ; and it triumphed.

While it lasted the fight was incredibly
fierce. "To be shunned and spat upon by
society, mobbed in public, and injured in one's
business—this was what it was to be an abolitionist." Abolitionism meant "self-renunciation
and social martyrdom." Garrison himself was
dragged through Boston with a rope round
his body and with difficulty was saved

from death; Elijah P. Lovejoy was killed while defending his printing press; Marius Robinson was tarred and feathered in Ohio; Amos Dresser got a flogging at Nashville for no fault; Whittier himself was beaten in the street and had his office in Philadelphia burned down by the mob; on another occasion the poet barely escaped with his life from a house in Concord, from the windows of which could be seen the murderous gleam of rifles in the moonlit street.

Whittier stepped into the fray with eyes open, in simple obedience to the direction of that " Light within " which he reverenced above all other; henceforth we shall see him as one,

Who, doomed to go in company with Pain,
And Fear, and Bloodshed, miserable train !
Turns his necessity to glorious gain.

In 1833 a National Anti-Slavery Convention met at Philadelphia on December 4th; Whittier attended, and like the other sixty-two delegates present, signed the famous Declaration drawn up by Garrison. Years after he wrote an interesting account of the proceedings, and drew graphic word portraits of many present; and there was this pleasing touch.—"In front of me, waking pleasant associations of the old homestead in the Merrimac Valley, sat my first school teacher, Joshua Coffin, the learned and worthy antiquarian and historian of Newbury."

The story of the great struggle in which Whittier was henceforth to bear his part, is to be found in its detail in Henry Wilson's "History of the Rise and Fall of the Slave Power." For most of us, however, it lives in the Quaker poet's lyrics. These Voices of Freedom thrill us yet, instinct with the "hate of hate, the scorn of scorn, the love of love." Their note was nobly struck in the first of them—the "Lines to William Lloyd Garrison."

> Champion of those who groan beneath
>   Oppression's iron hand.
>
>   ○   ○   ○
>
> I love thee with a brother's love,
>   I feel my pulses thrill,
> To mark thy spirit soar above

The cloud of human ill.
My heart hath leaped to answer thine
    And echo back thy words,
As leaps the warrior's at the shine
    And flash of kindred swords!

But Whittier's own grim attack was not long delayed. It came in a poem with no other title than " Stanzas," yet surely border ballad never broke forth with such a burden of wrath.

Our fellow-countrymen in chains!
    Slaves—in a land of light and law!
Slaves—crouching on the very plains
    Where rolled the storm of Freedom's war!
A groan from Eutaw's haunted wood,—
    A wail where Camden's martyrs fell,—
By every shrine of patriot blood,
    From Moultrie's wall and Jasper's well!

        ○   ○   ○

What, ho!—*our* countrymen in chains!
    The whip on WOMAN'S shrinking flesh!
Our soil yet reddening with the stains
    Caught from her scourging, warm and fresh
What! mothers from their children riven!
    What! God's own image bought and sold
AMERICANS to market driven,
    And bartered as the brute for gold!

Shall every flap of England's flag
  Proclaim that all around are free,
From "farthest Ind" to each blue crag
  That beetles o'er the Western Sea?
And shall we scoff at Europe's kings,
  When freedom's fire is dim with us,
And round our country's altar clings
  The damning shade of Slavery's curse?

Go—let us ask of Constantine
  To loose his grasp on Poland's throat;
And beg the lord of Mahmoud's line
  To spare the struggling Suliote,—
Will not the scorching answer come
  From Turbaned Turk, and scornful Russ:
"Go, loose your fettered slaves at home,
  Then turn, and ask the like of us!"

Nothing, perhaps, lent greater scorn to Whittier's lines than instances of the clergy gathering to lend their support to Slavery. In 1835, a great pro-Slavery meeting was held in Charleston, and the papers reported,—"The clergy of all denominations attended in a body, lending their sanction to the proceedings, and adding by their presence to the impressive character of the scene!"

Whittier's castigation came swiftly, and

with the inimitable force of righteous indignation.

Just God!—and these are they
Who minister at Thine altar, God of Right!
Men who their hands with prayer and blessing lay
    On Israel's Ark of light!

What! preach and kidnap men?
Give thanks,—and rob thy own afflicted poor?
Talk of Thy glorious liberty, and then
    Bolt hard the captive's door?

What! servants of Thy own
Merciful Son, who came to seek and save
The homeless and the outcast,—fettering down
    The tasked and plundered slave!

Pilate and Herod, friends!
Chief priests and rulers, as of old, combine!
Just God and holy! is that church, which lends
    Strength to the spoiler, Thine?

Paid hypocrites, who turn
Judgment aside, and rob the Holy Book
Of those high words of truth which search and burn
    In warning and rebuke;

Feed fat, ye locusts, feed!
And, in your tasselled pulpits, thank the Lord
That, from the toiling bondman's utter need,
    Ye pile your own full board.

How long, O Lord! how long
Shall such a priesthood barter truth away,

And in Thy name, for robbery and wrong
   At Thy own altars pray ?

As easily could the poet take up the heart-
cry of the slave, and compel currency for it
in the street and the home. Witness the
pathetic "Farewell of a Virginia slave-mother
to her daughters sold in bondage."—

    Gone, gone,—sold and gone,
     To the rice-swamp dank and lone.
  Where the slave-whip ceaseless swings,
  Where the noisome insect stings,
  Where the fever demon strews
  Poison with the falling dews,
  Where the sickly sunbeams glare
  Through the hot and misty air,—
    Gone, gone,—sold and gone,
     To the rice-swamp dank and lone,
    From Virginia's hills and waters,—
    Woe is me, my stolen daughters!

    Gone, gone,—sold and gone,
     To the rice-swamp dank and lone.
  There no mother's eye is near them,
  There no mother's ear can hear them ;
  Never, when the torturing lash
  Seams their back with many a gash,
  Shall a mother's kindness bless them,
  Or a mother's arms caress them.

Gone, gone,—sold and gone,
To the rice-swamp dank and lone,
From Virginia's hills and waters,—
Woe is me, my stolen daughters!

Gone, gone,—sold and gone,
To the rice-swamp dank and lone.
Oh, when weary, sad, and slow,
From the fields at night they go,
Faint with toil, and racked with pain,
To their cheerless homes again,
There no brother's voice shall greet them,—
There no father's welcome meet them.

Gone, gone,—sold and gone,
To the rice-swamp dank and lone,
From Virginia's hills and waters,—
Woe is me, my stolen daughters!

It was not always the stirring philippic, the biting satire, or the pathetic story of plantation miseries, that enlisted Whittier's pen. The martyrs of the cause, and those whom Death called from the fray, had their honoured names enshrined in these "Voices of Freedom." Thus the sudden death of Robert Rantoul, who died at his post in Congress, and with his last words protested in the name of Democracy against the Fugitive-Slave Law, evoked a noble tribute from the poet.

One day, along the electric wire,
　His manly word for freedom sped,
We came next morn : that tongue of fire
　Said only, "He who spake is dead."

c　　c　　c

Dead! he so great and strong and wise,
　While the mean thousands yet drew breath,
How deepened, through that dread surprise,
　The mystery and the awe of death!

But when sorrow has had vent, the needful trumpet blast awakes repiners to action :

Men of the North! your weak regret
　Is wasted here ; arise and pay
To freedom and to him your debt,
　By following where he led the way.

"The Branded Hand" relates to an instance of suffering for the cause—one among hundreds. Captain Jonathan Walker, a Massachussetts man, while working in Florida as a railway contractor, thought much on slavery, and treated those slaves with whom he had to deal with such humanity as to win their devotion. Not satisfied, he took seven of these poor fellows on a risky voyage to the West Indies, hoping to set them free. The party was captured,

and the brave captain pilloried, imprisoned,
and branded on his right hand with the letters
S.S. (signifying slave-stealer), and finally released
only on the payment of 150 dollars by his
Massachussetts friends.   The homecoming of
the gallant captain created a *furore* of joy,
and, as usual, Whittier put a song into the
mouths of the people, a right noble song.
Let critics call such outbursts mere "rhymed
eloquence" if they please; then let them remain unmoved by the written line, if they
can.

Welcome home again, brave seaman! with thy thoughtful brow and gray,
And the old heroic spirit of our earlier, better day,—
With that front of calm endurance, on whose steady
  nerve in vain
Pressed the iron of the prison, smote the fiery shafts
  of pain!

                  ○   ○

Why, that brand is highest honour!—than its traces
  never yet
Upon old armorial hatchments was a prouder blazon
  set;
And thy unborn generations, as they tread our rocky
  strand,

Shall tell with pride the story of their father's
    BRANDED HAND!

        o   o   o

Then lift that manly right-hand, bold ploughman of
    the wave!
Its branded palm shall prophesy, " SALVATION TO THE
    SLAVE!"
Hold up its fire-wrought language, that whoso reads
    may feel
His heart swell strong within him, his sinews change
    to steel.

Hold it up before our sunshine, up against our
    Northern air,—
Ho! men of Massachussetts, for the love of God,
    look there!
Take it henceforth for your standard, like the Bruce's
    heart of yore,
In the dark strife closing round ye, let that hand be
    seen before!

Who has not felt his heart beat double
to the march and meaning of words like
these :—

The voice of Massachussetts! Of her free sons and
    daughters,—
Deep calling unto deep aloud,—the sound of many
    waters!
Against the burden of that voice what tyrant power
    shall stand?
No fetters in the Bay State! No slave upon her land!

Look to it well, Virginians! In calmness we have
  borne,
In answer to our faith and trust, your insult and
  your scorn ;
You've spurned our kindest counsels, you've hunted
  for our lives,—
And shaken round our hearths and homes your manacles
  and gyves !

We wage no war,—we lift no arm,—we fling no torch
  within
The fire-damps of the quaking mine beneath your
  soil of sin ;
We leave ye with your bondmen, to wrestle, while
  ye can,
With the strong upward tendencies and god-like soul
  of man !

But for us and for our children, the vow which we
  have given
For freedom and humanity is registered in heaven ;
No slave-hunt in our borders,—no pirate on our strand!
No fetters in the Bay State,—no slave upon our land!

What a pen was this! that to-day was
hurriedly plied, and to-morrow millions were
stirred or stricken in their hearts. Whittier
had no rival, reply was impossible when he
smote, nor could any congeal the pitiful
tears he drew to eyes often unwilling to

weep. The effect of the lyrics can be but
half understood by us, for whom the events
of these years are blurred by time and distance.
Even in America, to-day, the younger generations have no conception of their first effects
on the public. "Tell your boys and girls,"
said Professor Thayer, of Harvard College,
to a teacher in the Friends' School in Providence, "tell your boys and girls, that however
much they admire and love Whittier, they
cannot know what a fire and passion of en-
thusiasm he kindled in the hearts of the little
company of Anti-slavery boys and girls of my
time, when they read his early poems."

It should be remembered that these songs
were written often in haste, and were with
equal haste printed as broadsides, or upon
cards, or were read at Anti-Slavery Meetings,
or sent to the newspapers. They were meant
to strike the iron while hot, to point a great
moral as the perception of it grew. They were
"the earnest and often vehement expression
of the writer's thought and feeling at critical

7

periods in the great conflict between Freedom
and Slavery . . they were protests, alarm-
signals, trumpet-calls to action." To these
words the poet added an acknowledgment of
what he conceived to be their artistic defects.

In 1838 Whittier came to Philadelphia to
resume those vexing cares of editorship, for
which he was, by his standard of health,
but ill fitted, yet from which no call of
duty might keep him back. Here we soon
find him in the thick of the fight,
editing the " Freeman."

No wonder if, heart-weary, he would now
and then leave the drouth and discord of
the city behind him in long country rambles.
In the following lines he strikes that chord
of longing for peace and the consolations of
green Nature which Matthew Arnold made his
own.

How bland and sweet the greeting of this breeze
        To him who flies
From crowded street and red walls weary gleam,

Till far behind him like a hideous dream
    The close dark city lies!

Here, while the market murmurs, while men throng
    The marble floor
Of Mammon's altar, from the crush and din
Of the world's madness let me gather in
    My better thoughts once more.

Oh, once again revive, while on my ear
    The cry of Gain
And low hoarse hum of Traffic die away,
Ye blessed memories of my early day
    Like sere grass wet with rain!—

Once more let God's green earth and sunset air
    Old feelings waken;
Through weary years of toil and strife and ill,
Oh, let me feel that my good angel still
    Hath not his trust forsaken.

Oftenest his steps would lead him out
to Frankford village, to Chalkley Hall, the
old residence of that "rare sea saint" he
had learned to revere at the home hearth.

Oh, far away beneath New England's sky,
    Even when a boy,
Following my plough by Merrimack's green shore,
His simple record I have pondered o'er
    With deep and quiet joy.

And hence this scene, in sunset glory warm,—
    Its woods around,
Its still stream winding on in light and shade,
Its soft, green meadows and its upland glade,—
    To me is holy ground.

He needed such moments. In Philadelphia untoward events were at hand. The Anti-slavery people had just built a meeting place, to which they gave the name of Pennsylvania Hall, and besides a large chamber for meetings, the building contained their book-store and the office of the "Freeman." The day of dedication came and went, and there had been no disturbance, but when on the second day an Anti-Slavery Convention of American Women was held, attended by some five hundred women, a mob was soon seething round the hall, and the speeches were made to the accompaniment of crashing windows. "Yet what," cried one speaker—the beautiful Angelina Grimké Weld, —"would the breaking of every window be? Any evidence that we are wrong, or that slavery is a good or wholesome institution? What if the mob should now burst in upon us, break up our meeting, and commit violence upon our persons — would this be anything compared with what the slaves endure?" It was thus that women championed their bond-sisters in those days.

The next morning there were more mobs and missiles, and in the evening the crisis arrived. What took place need not be related in detail, but the upshot was a bonfire for which the handsome hall and everything in it scarcely provided fuel to glut the mob with red flame and smoking ruins.

Outrages like these moved the Quaker poet to remembrance of his father's "days of bitterness," and thus, in his ear-compelling rhythms, old wrongs fought new, and evil was made once more to "justify the ways of God to men."

CHAPTER VI.

CONSCIOUS POWER.

"Know well, my soul, God's hand controls
Whate'er thou fearest ;
Round Him in calmest music rolls
Whate'er thou hearest.

What to thee is shadow, to Him is day,
And the end He knoweth,
And not on a blind and aimless way
The spirit goeth."
                                        "MY SOUL AND I."

"If the poet have this two-fold goodness,—the drill and the inspiration,—then he has health ; then he is a whole, and not a fragment ; and the perfection of his endowment will appear in his compositions."—EMERSON.

IN 1840 Whittier wrote to Joshua Leavitt,— "I have just returned to the quiet of my home, and have already barely had leisure to glance over the newspapers which have accumulated during my absence." He goes on to lament certain dissensions in the Anti-Slavery party which had arisen on the question as to how far political machinery ought to be used as a means to reformation. Whittier felt it his duty to exercise his right of citizenship at the ballot box in the cause of Liberty ; Garrison, with equal sincerity judged and counselled otherwise, and the result was a certain amount of coldness between the two. The controversy has lost its interest, but it made sad havoc at the time. In the end the old friendship was restored, and on Garrison's death, Whittier wrote, — " I choose rather with a feeling of gratitude to God, to recall the happiness of labouring with the noble company of whom Garrison was the central figure. I love to think of him as he seemed to me, when, in the fresh dawn of manhood, he sat with me in the old Haverhill farm-house, revolving even then schemes of benevolence . . . . and in all the varied scenes and situations where we acted together our parts in the great en- deavour and success of Freedom."

In 1840, the Haverhill homestead was

sold. Whittier's mother, sister, and aunt thereupon removed to Amesbury, a small town nine miles from Haverhill, with a population of about three thousand. The town is set on a hill side, beneath which the Merrimac glides, hardly more peacefully than did the years through which we are now to trace the poet's footsteps.

Let us see how the Whittier family circle stood at the time of this removal to Amesbury.

John Whittier, we know, had died at Haverhill in 1832, and Moses Whittier, the uncle, in 1824. Matthew Franklin, the poet's brother, was living in Boston, where he died so late as 1883. He was a clerk in the Naval Department of the Boston Custom House, where he is said to have been very popular on account of his humorous turn. He is described as having been "very different from his brother," but to have had the same love of seclusion. Mary, the elder sister, had been married some years to Mr. Jacob Caldwell, of Haverhill. Elizabeth and Aunt Mercy Hussey went to Amesbury with the mother.

But again the circle was broken in 1846, in which year Mercy Hussey died,—

> The sweetest woman ever Fate
> Perverse denied a household mate.

Elizabeth H. Whittier, the younger sister, lived till 1864, and was her brother's literary companion. She had a share of his genius, too, and Whittier included a few of her poems in his volume "Hazel Blossoms." She was also his co-worker in the Anti-Slavery cause, and on one occasion, at least, ran serious risk of violence at the hands of the mob.

From this time, Whittier's life was uneventful, and there is little to record but the sure development of his powers.

We have seen how in the flush of manhood he had secretly longed to "drink deep of the Pierian Spring." But for a poet, in whom genius was wedded to goodness, there could be no inspiration in the morning mists,

the river expanse, the eyes of village maidens,
nor in themes of home and legendary lore,
while the bitter cry of the slave was borne to
him on every breeze. His thought was
Coleridge's,—

> Was it right,
> While my unnumbered brethren toiled and bled,
> That I should dream away th' intrusted hours
> On rose-leaf beds, pampering the coward heart
> With feelings all too delicate for use?

Whittier we know, felt the disappointment
of his hopes.

> Oh not of choice, for themes of public wrong
> I left the green and pleasant paths of song.
> More dear to me some song of private worth,
> Some homely idyll of my native north.

Even his enlisted pen wandered when, in
moments of weariness, his thought would be,
"to the old paths my soul!" Thus, he writes—

> I know it has been said our times require
> No play of art, nor dalliance with the lyre,
> No weak essay with Fancy's chloroform
> To calm the hot, mad pulses of the storm,
> But the stern war-blast rather, such as sets
> The battle's teeth of serried bayonets,
> And pictures grim as Vernet's. Yet with these

Some softer tints may blend, and milder keys
Relieve the storm-stunned ear.   Let us keep sweet
If so we may, our hearts, even while we eat
The bitter harvest of our own device
And half-a-century's moral cowardice.

Whittier did keep his heart sweet, and when his "long harsh strife with strong-willed men" was over, he had won an abiding place in the hearts of his countrymen, who loved the poet the more because they had learned already to love the man.   It was in these strenuous years, when his Muse was handmaid to Social Reform, that Whittier won his un-contested title to be called the national poet.

The growth, then, of Whittier's poetical powers, after 1840, may be said to have been the unfolding of "the plan that pleased his boyish thought," modified, interrupted even, but also stimulated and deepened by those direct calls which suffering humanity continued to make upon his public sympathies.

Let us endeavour to follow in the main track of the poems, as year by year they added to the poet's fame.

In 1840, " Memories," quoted entire in another part of this book, was written, and, in the same year, " Merrimac," a poem in which the old feeling for quiet beauty and rural traditions brake forth unrestrainedly—

Home of my fathers!—I have stood
Where Hudson rolled his lordly flood :
Seen sunrise rest and sunset fade
Along his frowning Palisade ;
Looked down the Apalachian peak
On Juniata's silver streak ;
Have seen along his valley gleam
The Mohawk's softly winding stream ;
The level light of sunset shine
Through broad Potomac's hem of pine ;
And autumn's rainbow-tinted banner
Hang lightly o'er the Susquehauna ;
Yet wheresoe'er his step might be,
Thy wandering child looked back to thee!
Heard in his dreams thy river's sound
Of murmuring on its pebbly bound,
The unforgotten swell and roar
Of waves on thy familiar shore ;
And saw, amidst the curtained gloom
And quiet of his lonely room,
Thy sunset scenes before him pass.

In 1843 Whittier wrote one of his finest pieces, entitled " Follen." Charles Follen, a

young theologian and a friend of Whittier's,
had perished at sea, and after reading with
mournful interest an essay poor Follen had
written on the Future State, the poet's per-
plexed and sorrowing thoughts found vent in
this poem which, in lines like the following,
reminds us of "In Memoriam."

But be the prying vision veiled,
  And let the seeking lips be dumb,—
Where even seraph eyes have failed
  Shall mortal blindness seek to come.

We only know that thou hast gone,
  And that the same returnless tide
Which bore thee from us still glides on,
  And we who mourn thee with it glide.

On all thou lookest we shall look,
  And to our gaze ere long shall turn
That page of God's mysterious book
  We so much wish yet dread to learn.

With Him before whose awful power
  Thy spirit bent its trembling knee:—
Who in the silent greeting flower,
  And forest leaf ; looked out on thee,—

We leave thee with a trust serene,
  Which Time, nor Change, nor Death can move,
While with thy childlike faith we lean
  On Him whose dearest name is Love !

Other poems of 1843 were "Cassandra Southwick," a stirring Quaker ballad, "Chalkley Hall," and various "Voices of Freedom." These were followed in 1845 by a sheaf of Labour songs. In 1847 Whittier gave proof of the rapid growth of his powers in such pieces as "The Angels of Buena Vista," "Barclay of Ury," "My soul and I," "To my Sister," "Randolph of Roanoke," and "Proem."

The last named piece is prefixed to most editions of Whittier's poems; it shows how well Whittier understood his limitations as a poet.

Of mystic beauty, dreamy grace,
No rounded art the lack supplies ;
Unskilled the subtle lines to trace,
Or softer shades of Nature's face,
I view her common forms with unanointed eyes.

Nor mine the seer-like power to show
The secrets of the heart and mind ;
To drop the plummet-line below
Our common world of joy and woe,
A more intense despair or brighter hope to find.

Yet here at least an earnest sense
Of human right and weal is shown ;
    A hate of tyranny intense,
    And hearty in its vehemence,
As if my brother's pain and sorrow were my own.

"Barclay of Ury" is the great ballad of early Quakerism, and it will be well to quote it entire.

BARCLAY OF URY.

Up the streets of Aberdeen,
By the kirk and college green,
    Rode the Laird of Ury ;
Close behind him, close beside,
Foul of mouth and evil-eyed,
    Pressed the mob in fury.

Flouted him the drunken churl,
Jeered at him the serving-girl,
    Prompt to please her master ,
And the begging carlin, late
Fed and clothed at Ury's gate.
    Cursed him as he passed her.

Yet, with calm and stately mien,
Up the streets of Aberdeen
    Came he slowly riding :
And, to all he saw and heard,
Answering not with bitter word,
    Turning not for chiding.

Came a troop with broadswords swinging,
Bits and bridles sharply ringing,
   Loose and free and froward ;
Quoth the foremost, " Ride him down !
Push him ! prick him ! through the town
   Drive the Quaker Coward !"

But f rom out the thickening crowd
Cried a sudden voice and loud :
   "Barclay ! Ho ! a Barclay !"
And the old man at his side
Saw a comrade, battle-tried,
   Scarred and sunburned darkly ;

Who with ready weapon bare,
Fronting to the troopers there,
   Cried aloud : "God save us,
Call ye coward him who stood
Ankle-deep in Lutzen's blood,
   With the brave Gustavus ? "

"Nay, I do not need thy sword,
Comrade mine," said Ury's lord ;
   " Put it up, I pray thee :
Passive to His holy will,
Trust I in my Master still,
   Even though He slay me.

" Pledges of thy love and faith,
Proved on many a field of death,
   Not by me are needed."
Marvelled much that henchman bold,
That his laird, so stout of old,
   Now so meekly pleaded.

"Woe's the day!" he sadly said,
With a slowly shaking head,
    And a look of pity ;
"Ury's honest lord reviled,
Mock of knave and sport of child,
    In his own good city !

"Speak the word, and, master mine,
As we charged on Tilly's line,
    And his Walloon lancers,
Smiting through their midst we'll teach
Civil look and decent speech
    To these boyish prancers !"

"Marvel not, mine ancient friend,
Like beginning, like the end,"
    Quoth the Laird of Ury ;
"Is the sinful servant more
Than his gracious Lord who bore
    Bonds and stripes in Jewry ?

"Give me joy that in His name
I can bear, with patient frame,
    All these vain ones offer ;
While for them He suffereth long,
Shall I answer wrong with wrong,
    Scoffing with the scoffer ?

"Happier I, with loss of all,
Hunted, outlawed, held in thrall,
    With few friends to greet me,
Than when reeve and squire were seen,
Riding out from Aberdeen,
    With bared heads to meet me.

" When each goodwife, o'er and o'er,
Blessed me as I passed her door ;
      And the snooded daughter,
Through her casement glancing down,
Smiled on him who bore renown
      From red fields of slaughter.

" Hard to feel the stranger's scoff,
Hard the old friend's falling off,
      Hard to learn forgiving :
But the Lord His own rewards,
And His love with theirs accords,
      Warm and fresh and living.

"Through this dark and stormy night
Faith beholds a feeble light
      Up the blackness streaking ;
Knowing God's own time is best,
In a patient hope I rest
      For the full day-breaking ! "

So the Laird of Ury said,
Turning slow his horse's head
      Towards the Tolbooth prison,
Where, through iron grates, he heard
Poor disciples of the Word
      Preach of Christ arisen !

Not in vain, Confessor old,
Unto us the tale is told
      Of thy day of trial ;
Every age on him, who strays
From its broad and beaten ways
      Pours its sevenfold vial.

Happy he whose inward ear
Angel comfortings can hear,
　　O'er the rabble's laughter ;
And while Hatred's fagots burn,
Glimpses through the smoke discern
　　Of the good hereafter.

Knowing this, that never yet
Share of Truth was vainly set
　　In the world's wide fallow ;
After hands shall sow the seed,
After hands from hill and mead
　　Reap the harvests yellow.

Thus, with somewhat of the Seer,
Must the moral pioneer
　　From the future borrow ;
Clothe the waste with dreams of grain,
And, on midnight's sky of rain,
　　Paint the golden morrow !

In the years 1848, 1849, and 1850, some
remarkable poems appeared, including—" The
Slaves of Martinique," " The Curse of the
Charter Breakers," "Pæan," "The Crisis," "The
Men of Old," " Ichabod," all of which come
under the " Voices of Freedom." A keen
critic has boldly pronounced " Ichabod " " the
purest and profoundest *moral* lament in modern
literature, whether American or European. It

is the grief of angels in arms over a traitor brother, slain on the battle-field of heaven."

The nature of Whittier's work from 1850 to 1857 must be indicated in but a few words. Poems of self-examination and spiritual conflict are becoming numerous. Thus in " Questions of Life " the poet starts the old, old enigmas, the questionings of Job under the midnight heavens ; returning to God in the heart, and to the " simple heroic act by which he that believes *believes*."

In these years of increasing and conscious power appeared such fine poems as " First-Day Thoughts," "Tauler," " My Namesake," " Maud Muller," " The Barefoot Boy," " The Conquest of Finland," " The Panorama," " May Garvin," " Skipper Ireson's Ride," " The Last Walk in Autumn," " The Old Burying Ground," " Telling the Bees," and " The Palm Tree."

" Maud Muller " increased Whittier's reputation greatly, and may be said to have brought it across the Atlantic, for until this delightful ballad appeared, the poet's readers on this side had been few. Whittier was surprised by its success, and remarked to a friend— "If I had had any idea that it would have been so liked, I would have taken more pains with it." On the whole, looking at the perfection of this piece, we may be glad he did not labour it further.

Before passing to Whittier's best period a reference to the poem, "My Namesake," seems appropriate. This remarkable piece should be studied by the reader who desires insight into Whittier's character, for in it he reveals himself, as in "Proem" he discusses his work. A few verses must suffice :—

In him the grave and playful mixed
  And wisdom held with folly truce,
And Nature compromised betwixt
  Good fellow and recluse.

He loved his friends, forgave his foes ;
  And if their words were harsh at times
He spared his fellow men,—his blows
  Fell only on their crimes.

He loved the good and wise, but found
  His human heart to all akin,
Who met him on the common ground
  Of suffering and sin.

He had his share of care and pain,
  No holiday was life to him ;
Still in the heirloom cup we drain
  The bitter drop will swim.

Yet Heaven was kind, and here a bird
  And there a flower beguiled his way ;
And, cool, in summer noons, he heard
  The fountains plash and play.

On all his sad or restless moods
  The patient peace of Nature stole,
The quiet of the fields and woods
  Sank deep into his soul.

He worshipped as his fathers did,
  And kept the faith of childish days,
And, howsoe'er he strayed or slid,
  He loved the good old ways.

The simple tastes, the kindly traits,
  The tranquil air, and gentle speech,
The silence of the soul that waits
  For more than man to teach.

The cant of party, school, and sect,
  Provoked at times his honest scorn,
And Folly, in its grey respect,
  He tossed on satire's horn.

But still his heart was full of awe
And reverence for all sacred things ;
And, brooding over form and law,
He saw the Spirit's wings !

In 1857 Whittier's venerable mother died, aged 77. The poet's " filial attitude," says Mr. Underwood, "never changed from boyhood to maturity, and the tie was never loosened, . . the simplicity, truth, and trust of the early days remained to the last." But the poet's sorrow was soon to be drowned in the sorrows of his country.

CHAPTER VII.

THE MASTER YEARS.

"I mourn no more my vanished years :
    Beneath a tender rain,
An April rain of smiles and tears,
    My heart is young again.

The west-winds blow, and, singing low,
    I hear the glad streams run ;
The windows of my soul I throw
    Wide open to the sun.

No longer forward nor behind
    I look in hope or fear ;
But, grateful, take the good I find,
    The best of now and here.

I plough no more a desert land,
    To harvest weed and tare ;
The manna dropping from God's hand
    Rebukes my painful care.

I break my pilgrim staff,—I lay
    Aside the toiling oar ;
The angel sought so far away
    I welcome at my door."

                     "My Psalm."

"Establish thou the work of our hands upon us, yea
the work of our hands establish thou it."—Psalm xc., 17.

AT the end of the *fifties* the old stigma was
leaving the name of Abolitionist; politics
were disordered by the collapse of parties;

and the shadows of coming events fell black and ominous on the path of the disunited nation.

In 1861 the civil war broke out, and the Union was at stake. "The occasion," says Underwood, "lifted common men into heroes. The great souls whose lineaments are preserved in Plutarch's Lives might have been paralleled in many a shop or forge or farm-house. Life and treasure were of no value, but for the country's sake. The lover left his mistress, the husband his wife and children. Delicately nurtured men endured the fatigues, privations, and squalor of camp without murmur. Wounds, maiming, prisons, and hospitals were encountered as gaily as if they had been incidents of a holiday fête."

In Whittier's war pieces we trace the conflict of his feelings. So acute, indeed, was his suffering at this time, that any attempt to analyse his emotions must seem a profanation. He hated the War, he hated Slavery, yet the extinction of the one

seemed to depend on the continuance of the
other. Now he would indite a poem full
of expressions of trust in God, and of wist-
ful hopes of the end ; and now his pen
threw off ringing lines, whose possible effects
he scarcely paused to consider. Thus "Ein
feste Burg ist unser Gott" had hardly
appeared in the New York "Independent"
when it was heard in every marching column.
Lincoln said it was "just the kind of a
song I want the soldiers to hear." The last
three verses are these.

> Above the maddening cry for blood,
>   Above the wild war-drumming,
> Let Freedom's voice be heard, with good
>   The evil overcoming.
>   Give prayer and purse
>   To stay the Curse
>   Whose wrong we share,
>   Whose shame we bear,
>   Whose end shall gladden Heaven !
>
> In vain the bells of war shall ring
>   Of triumphs and revenges,
> While still is spared the evil thing
>   That severs and estranges.
>   But blest the ear

That yet shall hear
The jubilant bell
That rings the knell
Of Slavery for ever !

Then let the selfish lip be dumb,
    And hushed the breath of sighing ;
Before the joy of peace must come
    The pains of purifying.
        God give us grace
        Each in his place
        To bear his lot,
        And, murmuring not,
    Endure and wait and labour !

Whittier, it is certain, never wrote in favour of the war with intent ; but he was quite conscious of his sympathy with its picturesque incidents, and admiration of its multitudinous heroisms. In and above all, he trusted it would free the slave. It was said of him, " He was born a soldier and made into a Quaker, and the soldier knocks the Quaker down now and then." His own statement of the matter is much too interesting to be omitted here.

" Without intending any disparagement of

my peaceable ancestry for many generations, I have still strong suspicions that somewhat of the old Norman blood, something of the grim Berserker spirit, has been bequeathed to me. How else can I account for the intense childish eagerness with which I listened to the stories of old campaigners who sometimes fought their battles over again in my hearing? Why did I, in my young fancy, go up with Jonathan, the son of Saul, to smite the garrisoned Philistines of Michmash, or with the fierce son of Nun against the cities of Canaan? Why was Mr. Greatheart, in Pilgrim's Progress, my favourite character? What gave such fascination to the grand Homeric encounter between Christian and Apollyon in the valley? Why did I follow Ossian over Morven's battle-fields, exulting in the vulture-screams of the blind scald over his fallen enemies? Still later, why did the newspapers furnish me with subjects for hero-worship in the half-demented Sir Gregor McGregor, and Ypsilanti at the head of his knavish Greeks? I can only account for it on the supposition that the mischief was inherited,—an heirloom from the old sea-kings of the ninth century.

Education and reflection have indeed wrought a change in my feelings. The trumpet of the Cid, or Ziska's drum even, could not now waken that old martial spirit. . . It is only when a great thought incarnates itself in action, desperately striving to find utterance even in the sabre-clash and gun-fire, or when Truth and Freedom, in their mistaken zeal and mistrustful of their own powers, put on battle-harness, that I can feel any sympathy with merely physical daring."

During the War, the thirtieth annual meeting of the Anti-Slavery Society met at Philadelphia. Whittier, unable to attend, sent a letter, which Garrison read as from "one known and honoured throughout the civilised world." The letter is remarkable, as it shows how thoroughly Whittier appreciated the true extent of the work to be done. "For while," he wrote, "we may well thank God,

and congratulate one another on the prospect
of the speedy emancipation of the slaves of
the United States, we must not for a moment
forget that from this hour new and mighty
responsibilities devolve upon us to aid, direct,
and educate three millions, left free indeed,
but bewildered, ignorant, naked, and foodless
in the wild chaos of civil war. We have
to undo the accumulated wrongs of two
centuries ; to re-make the manhood that slavery
has well nigh unmade ; to see to it that the
long-oppressed coloured man has a fair field
for development and improvement, and to
tread under our feet the last vestige of that
hateful prejudice which has been the strongest
external support of Southern slavery. We
must lift ourselves at once to the true
Christian altitude, where all distinctions of
black and white are overlooked in the heart-
felt recognition of the brotherhood of man."

Then follows this deeply interesting personal
passage.

"I must not close this letter without

confessing that I cannot be sufficiently thank-
ful to the Divine Providence which, in a
great measure through thy instrumentality,
turned me so early away from what Roger
Williams calls, ' the world's great trinity,
pleasure, profit, and honour" to take side
with the poor and oppressed.   I am not insensible to literary reputation ; I love, perhaps,
too well the praise and good-will of my
fellow men ; but I set a higher value on
any name as appended to the Anti-Slavery
Declaration of 1833 than on the title page of
any book."   The President's Proclamation of
Abolition came with the New Year, and when
the Constitutional Amendment had ratified the
deed, and the bells rang out Emancipation
to the Slave, the poet's song broke for very
fulness into prayer and humiliation.

> Let us kneel :
> God's own voice is in that peal.
> And this spot is holy ground.
> Lord forgive us ! What are we,
> That our eyes this glory see,
> That our ears have heard the sound!

For the Lord
On the whirlwind is abroad ;
In the earthquake He has spoken ;
    He has smitten with His thunder
    The iron wall asunder,
And the gates of brass are broken !

    Loud and long
Lift the old exulting song ;
Sing with Miriam by the sea
    He has cast the mighty down ;
    Horse and rider sink and drown ;
"He hath triumphed gloriously ! "

    Did we dare,
In our agony of prayer,
Ask for more than he has done ?
    When was ever His right hand
    Over any time or land
Stretched as now beneath the sun ?

We will return to 1857. In this year
Whittier was invited by Phillips, Sampson &
Co., of Boston, to assist in the organization
of a new first-class periodical, favourable to
the great reforms, to be called "The Atlantic
Monthly." A brilliant staff of writers was
soon secured, including Emerson, Lowell, Longfellow, Oliver Wendell Holmes, Mrs. Stowe,
and other writers of the highest reputation.

A liberal scale of payment to contributors was adopted, and the new monthly succeeded from the first. Much of Whittier's finest work appeared in its columns, and quite recently it contained the venerable poet's last lines, written as a fraternal greeting to his old friend and fellow contributor, Oliver Wendell Holmes, on the attainment of his 83rd birthday.

While Whittier's pen was always at the service of the helpless and downtrodden, and was as a lance in his hand to do battle with evil, yet in his best years we see him gladly reverting to the literary ideals of his youth. There was no sacrificing of higher to lower work; the sacrifice had been all the other way; but there was an up-springing of suppressed life, and a joyful release from crowds and factions and city worries. It could not have been surprising if the old sweet inspirations had now failed, and the lyre broken when its strings were struck to slower measures.

But the poet had the dew of his youth; he cherished its memories too. The old familiar

walks by the sun-kissed Merrimac, the lake
of Kenoza with its finny droves of pickerel,
the salt sea meadows of Hampton, the glisten-
ing levels of wet beach encircling Salisbury,
the hills of Newbury rising out of farm lands
and nestling hamlets, the legends and runes
of local gossip, the village folk and their
quaint humours; all these had been with
him in

> Many an after year that rolled
> Heavily among mankind.

For Whittier was a poet to the core, and had
lived a strained life in cities. He had thought
nothing of his tastes when something higher was
concerned, but nevertheless he disliked public
life as such; he avoided society functions;
he wearied of the jangle of party strife; he
abominated war. Yet he had experienced
all these, and now could rest and review the painful journey. It is of himself he writes thus in "The Tent on the
Beach."

And one there was, a dreamer born,
  Who, with a mission to fulfil,
Had left the Muses' haunts to turn
  The crank of an opinion-mill,
Making his rustic reed of song
A weapon in the war with wrong,
Yoking his fancy to the breaking-plough
That beam-deep turned the soil for truth to spring
  and grow.

Too quiet seemed the man to ride
  The wingèd Hippogriff Reform ;
Was his a voice from side to side
  To pierce the tumult of the storm ?
A silent, shy, peace-loving man,
He seemed no fiery partisan
To hold his way against the public frown,
The ban of Church and State, the fierce mob's
  hounding down.

For while he wrought with strenuous will
  The work his hands had found to do,
He heard the fitful music still
  Of winds that out of dream-land blew.
The din about him could not drown
What the strange voices whispered down,
Along his task-field weird processions swept,
The visionary pomp of stately phantoms stepped.

The common air was thick with dreams,—
  He told them to the toiling crowd ;
Such music as the woods and streams

> Sang in his ear he sang aloud ;
> In still, shut bays, on windy capes,
> He heard the call of beckoning shapes,
> And, as the grey old shadows prompted him,
> To homely moulds of rhyme he shaped their legends
> grim.

In 1860, Whittier's calm home work bore fruit in a volume of " Home Ballads, Poems, and Lyrics." The first lines of the first poem, " The Witch's Daughter," are in the poet's new pastoral vein.

> It was the pleasant harvest time,
> When cellar-bins are closely stowed,
> And garrets bend beneath their load,
> And the old swallow-haunted barns—
> Brown-gabled, long, and full of seams
> Through which the moted sunlight streams,
> And winds blow freshly in, to shake
> The red plumes of the roosted cocks,
> And the loose hay-mow's scented locks—
> Are filled with summer's ripened stores,
> Its odorous grass and barley sheaves,
> From their low scaffolds to their eaves.

Whittier's art was consummate when he applied it to descriptions of familiar landscape and country life, and from the poems of his best period a collection of such gems might be made which for simple charm would stand nearly alone. This may seem a bold proposition, but where are we to easily match lines like these from the " Prophecy of Samuel Sewall."

I see, far southward, this quiet day,
The hills of Newbury rolling away,
With the many tints of the season gay,
Dreamily blending in autumn mist
Crimson, and gold, and amethyst.
Long and low, with dwarf trees crowned,
Plum Island lies, like a whale a-ground,
A stone's toss over the narrow sound.
Inland, as far as the eye can go,
The hills curve round like a bended bow ;
A silver arrow from out them sprung,
I see the shine of the Quasycung ;
And, round and round, over valley and hill,
Old roads winding, as old roads will,
Here to a ferry, and there to a mill ;
And glimpses of chimneys and gabled eaves,
Through green elm arches and maple leaves,—
Old homesteads sacred to all that can
Gladden or sadden the heart of man,—
Over whose thresholds of oak and stone
Life and Death have come and gone !
There pictured tiles in the fireplace show,

Great beams sag from the ceiling low,
The dresser glitters with polished wares,
The long clock ticks on the foot-worn stairs,
And the low, broad chimney shows the crack
By the earthquake made a century back.
Up from their midst springs the village spire
With the crest of its cock in the sun afire ;
Beyond are orchards and planting lands,
And great salt marshes and glimmering sands,
And, where north and south the coast-lines run,
The blink of the sea in breeze and sun !

Here we have description with few embellishments ; yet who does not feel the abiding charm of lines like these ?—

And, round and round, over valley and hill,
Old roads winding as old roads will,
Here to a ferry, and there to a mill.

Or take some joyous lines from the poem "Revisited," in which the poet apostrophises the laughing Merrimac.

Bring us the airs of hills and forests,
    The sweet aroma of birch and pine,
Give us a waft of the north-wind laden
    With sweetbrier odours and breath of kine !

Bring us the purple of mountain sunsets,
   Shadows of clouds that rake the hills,
The green repose of thy Plymouth meadows,
   The gleam and ripple of Campton rills.

Shatter in sunshine over thy ledges,
   Laugh in thy plunges from fall to fall ;
Play with thy fringes of elms, and darken
   Under the shade of the mountain wall.

The cradle-song of thy hillside fountains
   Here in thy glory and strength repeat ;
Give us a taste of thy upland music,
   Show us the dance of thy silver feet.

Such choice bits might be multiplied indefinitely. Does not the hot air seem to palpitate between the lines of this description of a midsummer day ?

The sky is hot and hazy, and the wind,
Wing-weary with its long flight from the south,
Unfelt ; yet, closely scanned, yon maple leaf
With faintest motion, as one stirs in dreams,
Confesses it. The locust by the wall
Stabs the noon-silence with his sharp alarm.
A single hay-cart down the dusty road
Creaks slowly with its driver fast asleep
On the load's top. Against the neighbouring hill,
Huddled along the stone wall's shady side,
The sheep show white, as if a snowdrift still

Defied the dog-star.   Through the open door
A drowsy smell of flowers—grey heliotrope,
And white sweet clover, and shy mignonette—
Comes faintly in, and silent chorus lends
To the pervading symphony of peace.

Whittier could put figures into his land-
scapes too ; he is a master-painter of village
life.   In the " Countess " we make acquaintance with—

The village folk, with all their humours quaint,
The parson ambling on his wall-eyed roan,
Grave and erect, with white hair backward blown ;
The tough old boatman, half amphibious grown ;
The muttering witch-wife of the gossip's tale,
And the loud straggler levying his black mail,—
Old customs, habits, superstitious fears,
All that lies buried under fifty years.

The poet, however, saw more than one
side of country life.   Here is a sketch which
may be contrasted with scenes depicted in
" Snow Bound," and it is just as fine.

I look
Across the lapse of half-a-century,
And call to mind old homesteads, where no flower
Told that the spring had come, but evil weeds,
Nightshade and rough-leaved burdock in the place

Of the sweet doorway greeting of the rose
And honeysuckle, where the house walls seemed
Blistering in sun, without a tree or vine
To cast the tremulous shadow of its leaves
Across the curtainless windows from whose panes
Fluttered the signal rags of shiftlessness ;
Within, the cluttered kitchen-floor, unwashed
(Broom-clean I think they called it) ; the best room
Stifling with cellar damp, shut from the air
In hot midsummer, bookless, pictureless
Save the inevitable sampler hung
Over the fireplace, or a mourning piece,
A green-haired woman, peony-cheek'd, beneath
Impossible willows ; the wide-throated hearth
Bristling with faded pine-boughs half concealing
The piled-up rubbish at the chimney's back :
And, in sad keeping with all things about them,
Shrill, querulous women, sour and sullen men,
Untidy, loveless, old before their time,
With scarce a human interest save their own
Monotonous round of small economies,
Or the poor scandal of the neighbourhood ;
Blind to the beauty everywhere revealed,
Treading the May-flowers with regardless feet ;
For them the song-sparrow and the bobolink
Sang not, nor winds made music in the leaves ;
For them in vain October's holocaust
Burned, gold and crimson, over all the hills,
The sacramental mystery of the woods.
Church-goers, fearful of the unseen Powers,
But grumbling over pulpit-tax and pew-rent,

Saving, as shrewd economists, their souls
And winter pork with the least possible outlay
Of salt and sanctity ; in daily life
Showing as little actual comprehension
Of Christian charity and love and duty
As if the Sermon on the Mount had been
Outdated like a last year's almanac :
Rich in broad woodlands and in half-tilled fields,
And yet so pinched and bare and comfortless,
The veriest straggler limping on his rounds,
The sun and air his sole inheritance,
Laughed at a poverty that paid its taxes,
And hugged his rags in self-complacency !

"Snow Bound," which was written in 1866, is the most distinctive and popular of Whittier's poems. It has been quoted so freely elsewhere in this book that it is needless to further illustrate its beauty.

"Skipper Ireson's Ride" was originally written wholly in the vernacular, but the poet adopted the extraordinary Marblehead dialect for the refrain, on the suggestion of a friendly critic.

Here's Flud Oirson, fur his horrd horrt
Torred an' futherr'd an' corr'd in a corrt
By the women o' Morble'ead.

"Abraham Davenport" is a fine blank

verse piece, founded on an incident of 1780.
" The 19th of May," says a local chronicler,
" was a remarkable day. Candles were lighted
in many houses ; the birds were silent and
disappeared, and the fowls retired to roost.
The legislature of Connecticut was then in
session at Hartford. A very general opinion
prevailed that the day of judgment was at
hand. The House of Representatives, being
unable to transact their business, adjourned.
A proposal to adjourn the Council was under
consideration. When the opinion of Colonel
Davenport was asked, he answered, ' I am
against an adjournment. The day of judgment is either approaching or it is not. If
it is not, there is no cause for an adjournment ; if it is, I choose to be found doing
my duty. I wish therefore that candles may
be brought.' "

And there he stands in memory to this day,
Erect, self-poised, a rugged face, half seen
Against the background of unnatural dark,
A witness to the ages as they pass
That simple duty hath no place for fear.

Abraham Davenport's grandfather was one of the founders of New Haven, a friend of the regicides, Goffe and Whalley, and first suggested the establishment of the college now called Yale : he was known by the Indians as ' so big study man.' "

If the writer were asked to name the poem in which he thinks Whittier's genius excels its every other effort, he would answer, " The Grave by the Lake." Others would think differently, but all must feel the wondrous spell of this poem. The impossibility of dealing with any large number of Whittier's finer poems suggests the propriety of quoting this piece entire, in conclusion of a chapter which could not, were it twice as long, do justice to Whittier's later work. It is founded upon the tradition that on the bank of Lake Winnepesauke, near the Melvin river, were found the bones of an Indian giant.

THE GRAVE BY THE LAKE.

Where the Great Lake's sunny smiles
Dimple round its hundred isles,
And the mountain's granite ledge
Cleaves the water like a wedge,
Ringed about with smooth, grey stones,
Rest the giant's mighty bones.

Close beside, in shade and gleam,
Laughs and ripples Melvin stream ;
Melvin water, mountain-born,
All fair flowers its banks adorn ;
All the woodlands voices meet,
Mingling with its murmurs sweet.

Over lowlands forest-grown,
Over waters, island-strown,
Over silver-sanded beach,
Leaf-locked bay and misty reach,
Melvin stream, and burial-heap,
Watch and ward the mountains keep.

Who that Titan cromlech fills ?
Forest kaiser, lord o' the hills ?
Knight who on the birchen tree
Carved his savage heraldry ?
Priest o' the pine-wood temples dim,
Prophet, sage, or wizard grim ?

Rugged type of primal man,
Grim utilitarian,
Loving woods for hunt and prowl,

Lake and hill for fish and fowl,
As the brown bear blind and dull
To the grand and beautiful :

Not for him the lesson drawn
From the mountains smit with dawn.
Star-rise, moon-rise, flowers of May,
Sunset's purple bloom of day,—
Took his life no hue from thence,
Poor amid such affluence ?

Haply unto hill and tree
All too near akin was he :
Unto him who stands afar
Nature's marvels greatest are ;
Who the mountain purple seeks
Must not climb the higher peaks.

Yet who knows in winter tramp,
Or the midnight of the camp,
What revealings faint and far,
Stealing down from moon and star,
Kindled in that human clod
Thought of destiny and God ?

Stateliest forest patriarch,
Grand in robes of skin and bark,
What sepulchral mysteries,
What weird funeral-rites, were his ?
What sharp wail, what drear lament,
Back scared wolf and eagle sent ?

Now, whate'er he may have been,
Low he lies as other men ;
On his mound the partridge drums,

There the noisy blue-jay comes ;
Rank nor name nor pomp has he
In the grave's democracy.

Part thy blue lips, northern lake !
Moss-grown rocks, your silence break !
Tell the tale, thou ancient tree !
Thou, too, slide-worn Ossipee !
Speak, and tell us how and when
Lived and died this king of men !

Wordless moans the ancient pine ;
Lake and mountain give no sign ;
Vain to trace this ring of stones ;
Vain the search of crumbling bones :
Deepest of all mysteries,
And the saddest, silence is.

Nameless, noteless, clay with clay
Mingles slowly day by day ;
But somewhere, for good or ill,
That dark soul is living still ;
Somewhere yet that atom's force
Moves the light-poised universe.

Strange that on his burial-sod
Harebells bloom, and golden-rod.
While the soul's dark horoscope
Holds no starry sign of hope !
Is the Unseen with sight at odds
Nature's pity more than God's ?

Thus I mused by Melvin's side,
While the summer eventide
Made the woods and inland sea

And the mountains mystery ;
And the hush of earth and air
Seemed the pause before a prayer,—

Prayer for him, for all who rest
Mother Earth, upon thy breast,—
Lapped on Christian turf, or hid
In rock-cave or pyramid :
All who sleep, as all who live,
Well may need the prayer, " Forgive."

Desert-smothered caravan,
Knee-deep dust that once was man,
Battle-trenches ghastly piled,
Ocean-floors with white bones tiled,
Crowded tomb and mounded sod,
Dumbly crave that prayer to God.

Oh the generations old
Over whom no church-bells tolled,
Christless, lifting up blind eyes
To the silence of the skies !
For the innumerable dead
Is my soul disquieted.

Where be now these silent hosts ?
Where the camping-ground of ghosts ?
Where the spectral conscripts led
To the white tents of the dead ?
What strange shore or chartless sea
Holds the awful mystery ?

Then the warm sky stooped to make
Double sunset in the lake ;
While above I saw with it,

Range on range, the mountains lit ;
And the calm and splendour stole
Like an answer to my soul.

Hear'st thou, O of little faith,
What to thee the mountain saith,
What is whispered by the trees ?—
"Cast on God thy care for these ;
Trust Him, if thy sight be dim :
Doubt for them is doubt of Him.

" Blind must be their close-shut eyes
Where like night the sunshine lies,
Fiery-linked the self-forged chain
Binding ever sin to pain,
Strong their prison-house of will,
But without He waiteth still.

" Not with hatred's undertow
Doth the Love Eternal flow ;
Every chain that spirits wear
Crumbles in the breath of prayer ;
And the penitent's desire
Opens every gate of fire.

" Still Thy love, O Christ arisen,
Yearns to reach these souls in prison !
Through all depths of sin and loss
Drops the plummet of Thy cross !
Never yet abyss was found
Deeper than that cross could sound ! "

Therefore well may Nature keep
Equal faith with all who sleep,
Set her watch of hills around

Christian grave and heathen mound,
And to cairn and kirkyard send
Summer's flowery dividend.

Keep, O pleasant Melvin stream,
Thy sweet laugh in shade and gleam!
On the Indian's grassy tomb
Swing, O flowers, your bells of bloom!
Deep below, as high above,
Sweeps the circle of God's love.

CHAPTER VIII.

SUNDOWN.

I have but Thee, my Father! let Thy spirit
  Be with me then to comfort and uphold;
No gate of pearl, no branch of palm I merit,
  Nor street of shining gold.

Suffice it if—my good and ill unreckoned,
  And both forgiven through Thy abounding grace—
I find myself by hands familiar beckoned
  Unto my fitting place.

Some humble door among Thy many mansions,
  Some sheltering shade where sin and striving cease,
And flows for ever through heaven's green expansions,
  The river of Thy peace.

There, from the music round about me stealing,
  I fain would learn the new and holy song,
And find at last, beneath Thy trees of healing,
  The life for which I long.

"AT LAST."

———

"I have never desired or hoped to found a school of
poetry, nor even written with the definite object of in-
fluencing others to follow my example: I have only written
as the spirit came and went, often unable to give utterance to the best poems that were in my heart, the utterance being holden; but it has been the crowning joy of a
prolonged old age that my life has not been entirely
valueless, and that I have been allowed to see the end of
slavery in my country."

J. G. WHITTIER. (From a letter.)

WHITTIER'S later years were spent in the
      seclusion of his homes at Amesbury and
at Oak Knoll, and were cheered by the visits
and attentions of innumerable friends and

admirers. It is not in the writer's power to give a personal sketch of Whittier at first hand, nor does he propose to quote any of the more or less lengthy sketches which have been written by some who have had personal relations with the poet. Whittier's ban is against the inclusion of such matter, if we are to take as literally meant the following verses from "My Namesake,"—

Let Love's and Friendship's tender debt
   Be paid by those I love in life,
Why should the unborn critic whet
   For me his scalping knife?

Why should the stranger peer and pry
   One's vacant house of life about,
And drag for curious ear and eye
   His faults and follies out?

Why stuff, for fools to gaze upon
   With chaff of words, the garb he wore,
As corn-husks when the ear is gone
   Are rustled all the more?

Let kindly Silence close again,
   The picture vanish from the eye,
And on the dim and misty main
   Let the small ripple die.

One event which brightened Whittier's last years should be mentioned here. On his seventieth birthday (December 17th, 1877), at the Hotel Brunswick, in Boston, a brilliant band of literary men sat down to a dinner given by the publishers of the "Atlantic Monthly" in honour of the Quaker poet and patriot. About seventy guests were present, and, near the poet, there sat at the table Emerson and Longfellow. Whittier made no speech but contributed these lines, which were read by Longfellow :

Beside that milestone where the level sun
Nigh unto setting, sheds his last, low rays
On word and work irrevocably done,
Life's blending threads of good and ill outspun,
I hear, O friends ! Your words of cheer and praise,
Half doubtful if myself or otherwise,
Like him in the old Arabian joke,
A beggar slept and crownèd Caliph woke.
Thanks not the less. With not unglad surprise
I see my life-work through your partial eyes ;
Assured, in giving to my home-taught songs
A higher value than of right belongs,
You do but read between the written lines
The finer grace of unfulfilled designs.

John Greenleaf Whittier died on September
7th of this year, 1892, aged 85 years.

Those who have read even this slight
sketch through, will need no summary of the
characteristic qualities which endeared Whittier
to his countrymen, to his near friends, and
to his fellow members of the Society of
Friends on both sides of the Atlantic. They
are enshrined in his poetry whose simple
melodies will haunt the ears of men in years
to come, and when these have grown faint
and far, the good he did will have passed
into the constitution of our world, adding its
energy to the broadening stream that makes
for righteousness in men and nations.

For himself, let the poet's own words of
retrospect suffice.—

Poor and inadequate the shadow-play
Of gain and loss, of waking and of dream,
  Against life's solemn background needs must seem
At this late hour. Yet, not unthankfully,
I call to mind the fountains by the way,
The breath of flowers, the bird-song on the spray,
Dear friends, sweet human loves, the joy of giving

And of receiving, the great boon of living
  In grand historic years when Liberty
Had need of word and work, quick sympathies
For all who fail and suffer, song's relief,
Nature's uncloying loveliness ; and chief,
  The kind restraining hand of Providence,
  The inward witness, the assuring sense
Of an Eternal Good which overlies
The sorrow of the world, Love which outlives
All sin and wrong, Compassion which forgives
To the uttermost, and Justice whose clear eyes
Through lapse and failure look to the intent,
And judge our frailty by the life we meant.

THE END.

HEADLEY BROS
INVICTA
PRINTING WORKS

ASHFORD · KENT